I0690575

BRUISED FRUIT

First Edition

Published by The Nazca Plains Corporation
Las Vegas, Nevada
2010

ISBN: 978-1-61098-023-4
Ebook: 978-1-61098-021-1

Published by

The Nazca Plains Corporation ®
4640 Paradise Rd, Suite 141
Las Vegas NV 89109-8000

PUBLISHER'S NOTE
Bruised Fruit is a work of fiction created wholly by *Robin Anderson's*
imagination. All characters are fictional and any resemblance to any
persons living or deceased is purely by accident. No portion of this
book reflects any real person or events.

Fish Photo, Ultrapro
Male Mannequin, K. Özcan Keles
Fish Bowl, Eric Isselée

Art Director, Blake Stephens

DEDICATION

For Bob Miller

Maybe even more memories!

BRUISED FRUIT

First Edition

Robin Anderson

CONTENTS

PROLOGUE

Somewhere in England – 1998

Unlike most small boys, Jeremy Spiers didn't get a thrill from pulling the wings off flies, he much preferred cutting off the legs of frogs, or – when he could find a suitable nest – pulling off the heads from straining, open-mouthed fledglings as they blindly stretched out for mummy bird's expected worm. Frying his pet white mice was another source of unexpected fun. Fortunately these bred so quickly there always seemed to be an adequate supply for this sporadic ritual. There were, however, two setbacks to this little game. One; it could only be instigated when everyone was conveniently away from the house and two; there followed the tedious task of having to clean the frying pan, a chore not very efficiently performed by Master Spiers.

Jasmine, the black lackadaisical West Indian cleaner continually blamed Mr Jeremy senior for this wrongdoing (he was well-known by the long suffering woman for his messy snacking). 'Why dat man mus' always fry dem sausages instead of neva' usin' da grill I'll neva' know!' she would loudly complain. Jeremy's extra curriculum activities had been temporarily put on hold when, in an extra burst of enthusiasm and ingenuity, he'd cut off the tail of the neighbour's new

Labrador puppy. The severely chastised young boy argued vehemently that this was done out of concern and without a malicious motive.

'I thought little Boris was a cocker Spaniel!' Jeremy had cried in defiance to the reprimand received, 'and all cockers have short tails!' An added touch of brilliance to his case was Boris's future embarrassment at not having had his tail docked as a puppy. 'It could lead to him developing a complex,' he had tearfully hiccupped.

Impressed by Jeremy junior's sensitivity as to Boris's future feelings, his proud parents, in a form of mollification to the pup's distraught owners for the misdemeanour, banned the contrite little boy from using his play station for what seemed to be a never-ending week. Revenge, in the case of the six year olds' irritation at his parents' attitude, was not 'a dish best served cold' but a dish served hot, 212 degrees Fahrenheit hot. Jeremy simply – and with great glee - added a kettle of boiling water to his sister's pet goldfish bowl. Her endless, confused tears as to how her two 'fishies' ended up lifeless and floating on the steaming surface served only as a momentary appeasement for him. To Jeremy's ever active and very imaginative mind, boiling his sister's fish was simply not vengeful enough. It was while sitting in the loft and playing with his 'pee pee' – this always gave a delicious tickling sensation and one he seemed to find more and more apparent when indulging in his unlikely 'hobbies' – Jeremy came (mentally, not literally) upon the idea which would make all his previous endeavours of torture (he viewed these as fun) seem tame by comparison.

Still secretly savouring his first gratification (and pee pee stimulation) at discovering revenge a better dish when bubbling hot as opposed to depressingly cold, Jeremy made the decision there and then; no play station had led to pain station with the young boy being severely put out. What had worked for little sisters 'fishies' would be even bettered. Jeremy, also having practised on his mice, saw no reason why not to cook his tedious, tiresome and restraining parents. The plan went even better than expected. A sleeping Hugo and Daphne Spiers plus little Emily and her new goldfish were suitably barbecued and boiled when the house mysteriously burned down.

A traumatised Jeremy – his escape was described by the tabloids as 'miraculous' – had later been found wandering barefoot and bewildered along a nearby street. The tearful little boy, wearing only his pyjama bottoms and clutching a well-worn (and obviously much loved) teddy bear won the nation's heart by asking in a choking, little voice, 'Where are Mummy and Daddy and Emmie? Benjie and me can't find them...'

Jeremy was immediately taken in by a distraught Uncle David - Hugo's brother, a vicar – and Sybil, his nervous, neurotic wife. The childless couple welcomed the new little orphan into their simple, Spartan home with open arms. As Sybil whispered, clutching his thin, shaking frame to her ample, squishy bosom and sniffing loudly into his mop of curly blond hair, 'We always wanted a little boy of our own and in His strange way but with His usual infinite wisdom God has given us *you*!'

Jeremy's fertile almost seven year old mind had gone into overdrive. As he confided to Benjie one evening a few months later –the two were in his tiny bed and had just played a hearty game of "rubadub rub" or "pee pee tickles" which meant Jeremy would rub the teddy bear up and down on his increasingly sprightly and sensitive acorn-like penis – 'Aunt Sybil's very nasty, Benjie, and her breath smells. Jasmine always used to put that stuff from a blue plastic bottle down the loo for the smell. I wonder if there some of this here in the vicarage..?" Before he could hear Benjie's reply Jeremy had drifted off into a blissful sleep, a small smile playing on his cherubic lips.

Jeremy was to find the bottle of household bleach the next day.

CHAPTER 1

'Jeremy dear,' chirruped Aunt Sybil 'Auntie has a surprise for you today…a new *friend*! Come and say hello to Tiffany and Tiffany's mummy who is *auntie's* friend, Mrs Cowper!'

Jeremy looked at the shy little girl smiling coyly at from behind the formidable Mrs Cowper. 'Hello Jeremy,' said Mrs Cowper in an over bright voice (she'd obviously been told the reason for his being there), 'please call me Auntie Di…' she gave a girlish giggle, causing her large, soft frame (similar to Aunt Sybil's) to wobble. 'It's Tiffany's daddy, your new Uncle Edward, who's responsible for our special names. We're Uncle Edward's jewels, you see, Tiffany after the jewellers and because she's her daddy's little jewel. I'm Di – short for Diana – because he sees me as his *diamond*!'

'Oh Di!' squeaked Aunt Sybil, equally as girlish. 'You are a one!'

'A diamond, you mean?' trilled Mrs Cowper, setting the two off in a further paroxysm of giggles.

Jeremy looked up at the two women aghast and then back at the still hiding Tiffany who, to his utter amazement, suddenly stuck out a small, bright pink precociously pointed tongue at him. More to his amazement was the sudden tingle in his pee pee on the sighting the pert, pink protuberance.

'Hello Tiffany,' he said in his sweet, choirboy-like voice and 'How do you do, Auntie Di, I'm so pleased to meet you.'

'Oh,' said Mrs Cowper, totally charmed by the cherubic little boy. 'They certainly were correct when they said manners maketh a little man!' She gave another giggle and clutched her ample bosoms. 'And we're both so pleased to meet you too, Jeremy! Aren't we Tiffany?' she cooed.

Tiffany's response was another showing of the disturbing, pee pee tingling little pink tongue.

Smiling over-brightly Aunt Sybil paused momentarily before making what appeared to be – for her – an earth shattering decision. 'Why not take Tiffany into the garden and show her your new swing?' she carolled before turning to a still beaming Mrs Cowper. 'Uncle David and I bought it as a "welcome" gift for Jeremy. He simply *adores* it!'

'A swing? What *fun!*' exclaimed Mrs Cowper. She turned to a now scowling Tiffany and an even more scowling Jeremy. 'Doesn't a swing sound fun, Tiffany?' Her large head swivelled on her large neck to face Jeremy. 'Don't push Tiffany too high,' she warned laughingly. 'You look such a strong little boy!'

'Yes, show Tiffany your swing while Auntie Di and Auntie Sybil get the tea ready.' Aunt Sybil gave the two children a saccharine smile. 'I have meringues and chocolate 'éclairs,' she chirruped, 'so work up a nice appetite the two of you!'

Still scowling, Jeremy led the little girl through from the kitchen to the neat back garden. The swing in question stood in spindly silence in front of them.

'I hate swings,' said Tiffany in her high, flute-like voice. 'They're like doggie pooh. They stink!' With that she again stuck out her tantalising little tongue, this time at the object of her derision.

Jeremy had no alternative but to fall instantly in love.

'But,' added the little girl, turning and looking directly with her widened, bright blue eyes at the now red-faced little boy, a small, sly smile appearing on her angelic face. 'If you push me very high you can see my knickers!'

Jeremy gulped. He'd never seen a real live girl's knickers before. He'd certainly seen photographs of ladies in frilly ones and tiny ones in magazines Daddy Hugo had kept in the bottom drawer of his desk in his study (as did Uncle David, under a pile of parish papers), but to see these in situ – as if it were – would be a first. He gave another gulp. 'Get on the swing then,' he said without any show of chivalry. 'What colour are they?' he added unnecessarily as Tiffany clambered on to the wooden swing seat.

'Wait and see' she trilled, wriggling and settling herself comfortably on the seat. 'And then,' she added with an even slyer smile, 'you can show me yours!'

'Boys don't wear knickers!' retorted Jeremy turning an even deeper rapid crimson. 'Boys wear underpants.'

'See if I care!' chortled Tiffany. 'Pants, ants, knickers, snickers! As long as you show them to me!'

The anticipation of seeing under Tiffany's dress took precedence over any embarrassment. 'Oh, OK then,' Jeremy said resignedly. 'But we'll have to go into the garden shed, I'm not taking off my trousers here in the garden.' He lowered his voice conspiratorially. 'We don't want my aunt and your mother seeing us, now do we?'

Tiffany nodded her head in agreement, her blonde curls bouncing.

'OK, hold on then while I push. When you are at your highest I'll run round to the front!' Nodding again, the little girl held on tightly as the little boy duly pushed. Satisfied that the swing was at its highest, Jeremy dashed round to the front. A laughing Tiffany sailed up above him, her tiny legs held firmly together as were her pointed toes. Jeremy stopped pushing.

'Whatsamatter?' demanded the little girl, giving him a glare. 'Why have you stopped?'

'Because, like all girls, you cheated!' sniped the little boy. 'You kept your legs together and I couldn't see your knickers! So you needn't think I'm going to show you my underpants!'

'Well I can hardly swing on the swing with my legs wide open, can I?' Tiffany snapped back. '*Everyone* keeps their legs together on a swing, even boys!' The latter being said with a definite tone of scorn.

'Well why did you say I could see your knickers then?'

'I didn't know you wouldn't!' came the tart reply. 'But,' she added sotto voce 'I can still show them to you in the shed...'

'OK,' said Jeremy, his voice trembling. 'Follow me.'

Inside the musty, little-used shed the two children stood looking at each other. 'You first,' said Tiffany.

'No,' said Jeremy. 'You first. After all, I was going to see your knickers on the swing before you saw my underpants.'

'See if I care,' said Tiffany with another toss of her curls. Without further ado she rustled up her dress and proudly displayed her plain white cotton knickers. 'Now you.' She instructed.

Giving a loud swallow, Jeremy dropped his shorts. To his chagrin it was at that very moment that his pee pee began to develop a strange tingle. Meanwhile Tiffany was curiously eyeing his little bump. 'You're not flat like me.' She observed.

'Of course I'm not flat,' said Jeremy. 'I've got a pee pee. All boys have a pee pee.' He looked at the face of the puzzled little girl before dropping his eyes to the very flat surface at the start of her legs. 'Of course,' he said with a definite smirk. 'Girls don't have pee pees. You have *holes*!'

'I'd rather have a hole than a bump,' said Tiffany. She peered again at Jeremy's little lump. 'It looks rather like a nose!'

'It's nothing like a nose,' said Jeremy crossly. 'It's like a pipe. Look.' With that he pulled down his pants to prove his point.

'Ugh! It looks exactly like a pink worm!' said the little girl. 'A worm with a knot!' she added leaning closer to peer at the tiny curly foreskin.

'Better than a *hole*!' retorted the little boy. 'C'mon then, fair's fair, I've shown you my pee pee now show me your hole.'

Without hesitation Tiffany did as requested.

It was now Jeremy's turn to lean forward and peer. 'It's not a hole,' he said crossly. 'It's a slit!' Before an angry Tiffany could respond he'd taken his finger and given her a hefty prod in between her labia.

'Ouch! Stop it! That hurt!' cried the little girl. To get her own back she promptly pinched his tiny penis.

'Ow!' squawked Jeremy and promptly stuck his forefinger back into the startled girl.

'Jeremy? Tiffany?' Aunt Sybil's high pitched voice broke into Jeremy's second squawk as Tiffany promptly pinched him back. 'Tea's ready. Where are you?' The voice had taken on an anxious tone. 'Jeremy? Tiffany?'

'We're here!' called Jeremy. 'I was just showing Tiffany the spiders' webs in the shed.' With a cunning flash of ingenuity he quickly added. 'Like all girls she said she's afraid of spiders and I told her not to be so silly.' He gave a wicked chortle. 'She even touched a web!'

'It was nasty!' carolled Tiffany, giving him a wicked grin.

'Well, stop playing with those nasty spiders' webs and come and wash your hands,' commanded Aunt Sybil. The two now giggling children could hear her complaining to Aunt Di. 'Why is it that *all* children seem to enjoy getting deliberately grubby?'

'Where were they?' questioned Aunt Di.

'In the garden shed.' There was a pause. 'Oh no, I wouldn't think anything untoward,' came the reassuring response. 'After all, they're only children. I'm sure it was all purely innocent,' said Aunt Sybil.

A smiling Tiffany and Jeremy, hands duly washed, joined the grownups at the kitchen table.

'Mmmmm!' said Tiffany nibbling on the end of her éclair.

'Mmmmm!' said Jeremy nibbling on his meringue. He eyed Tiffany who had stopped in the middle of her nibbling and who gave him a sudden chocolaty smile, her eyes crinkling. The young boy gave an equally meringue enhanced smile in return. Tiffany wickedly slid out her brown smeared tongue. Jeremy gave a gulp and began to choke and splutter.

'Oh dear!' cried Aunt Sybil, patting his back. 'Something go down the wrong way? Here, take a sip of your orange juice.'

That night in bed playing 'pee pee tickles' with a compliant Benjie, Jeremy's mind was fixedly dwelling on the sight of Tiffany's pointed pink chocolate coated tongue. Suddenly casting Benjie aside he gave the aforesaid pee pee a painful pinch. 'Ooh,' he squeaked. 'Ooh!'

Over breakfast the next morning Jeremy announced that Tiffany was his new best friend.

'Oh, I'm so pleased!' cried his aunt, delighted that the glamorous, classy Mrs Cowper's little girl had made such a hit with her strange, reclusive nephew. 'Isn't it fun, David? Jeremy's made a new friend with Di's Tiffany.'

'Hmmph!' responded his uncle from behind the weekly Church Times.

'Can I see her again? Today?' asked the little boy.

'Well, maybe not today,' answered his aunt diplomatically. 'But I'll speak to Auntie Di and arrange something during the week.' She smiled indulgently at the young boy smiling back with an angelic expression on his innocent 'butter wouldn't melt in his mouth' face.

'Goody!' said Jeremy. ''Cos I *like* Tiffany. She's not soppy like other girls.'

'And that's all because of *you*, Jeremy, teaching her not to be afraid of spiders!' Aunt Sybil poured another cup of tea for herself and Uncle David. 'More juice, darling?' She smiled benevolently at her still smiling nephew.

'No thank you,' said the little boy. 'May I get down, please?'

'Of course,' smiled Sybil, adding, 'and as it's Saturday and you have no school Uncle David thought you may like to join him for when he goes into town. He's got a meeting with a parishioner but you can easily be dropped off at the local market. In fact,' – Aunt Sybil looked as if she had just had the most amazing brainwave – 'why don't I see if Aunt Di and Tiffany can't meet you there? They always go to the Saturday market.'

'Yes please!' enthused Jeremy. 'That would be lovely.'

Within minutes Aunt Sybil had been on the phone to Auntie Di. Sadly she and Tiffany wouldn't be going to the market this particular

Saturday but Jeremy was more than welcome to come along and spend the morning at their house.

'Lovely.' said Jeremy.

The Cowpers lived in a sombre, large Victorian house on the outskirts of the village. The house, built for a former wealthy industrialist and arrogantly named 'The Manor', was set in what the owners deemed 'a park' of some forty acres. Access was via a pair of formidable electrically controlled wrought iron gates leading to a long winding tarmac drive. Tall rhododendron bushes and a neat privet hedge flanked the curving road ending up in a large forecourt.

'Are the Cowpers very rich?' questioned Jeremy, looking open-mouthed at the towering, ugly red brick edifice in front of them, it's black slate roof positively bristling with a multitude of chimney stacks. Uncle David smiled benignly at his small nephew sitting alongside him in the vicarage Mondeo. 'Some people are blessed,' he said in his hollow tenor. He gave the little boy's knee a squeeze. 'As are we with our new son,' he added, his pale lashes fluttering momentarily towards the sun visor.

'Yes, but are they rich?' repeated the little boy.

'Very,' said Uncle David with just a touch of irritation. He turned off the ignition. 'Mr Cowper owns a group of jewellery shops.' With an unexpected show of venom he added with a strange twisting of his mouth. 'Their real name was Kupper but they changed it to Cowper.'

'Why, uncle?'

'Because they're ashamed of being er...Jewish.'

'What's Jewish?'

'Different to us Christians,' said Uncle David, somewhat uncomfortably.

'How?'

David Spiers gave his nephew's tiny knee a further squeeze as a sudden inspiration – or divine light as he was later to say to a blushing Aunt Sybil – came to him. 'Well, young Jeremy, you know that at the end of your willie...er, your pee thing, you have a little hat, or tassel?' Jeremy nodded, beginning to go pink again. Surely grownups didn't talk about such things, fascinating as they may be? 'Like your daddy had and like I have?' continued his uncle now getting carried away and, to his horror, beginning to feel a growing response in his groin. 'Jewish men and boys don't. They have them cut off when they are babies.'

'Oh,' said Jeremy. He gave his uncle – Uncle David had now gone a bright red himself – an even more curious look. 'Why? And doesn't it hurt?'

'Ah, look! Here's Auntie Di and your new best friend Tiffany!' cried a relieved David Spiers glancing through the windscreen. 'Good morning! Good morning!' he cried bluffly. 'Sorry we remained sitting in the car. Young Jeremy and I were having a "man to man" discussion!' He gave another blustery laugh. 'You look well, Di and look at you, young Tiffany, don't you look pretty today with that bright bow in your hair!' Getting out of the car he turned and tapped on the window. 'Out you get, young Jeremy.' He gestured vaguely at Di and a staring Tiffany. 'I'll be back within about two hours, if that's not too much trouble…' He gave an embarrassed laugh. 'Although I'm sure Tiffany and David will find lots to do and time will simply fly by!'

'Why doesn't Jeremy stay for lunch?' suggested Auntie Di. 'Parsons, our driver, can bring him back to the vicarage later.'

'Would you like that, Jeremy?' smiled his uncle, inwardly delighted that their 'son' had been invited to lunch at 'The Manor,' even though an impromtu one.

'Oh yes,' answered the little boy, his face lighting up. Not only was he going to stay for lunch but he was also going to ask Tiffany for a second viewing of her little slit as well as ask about her father's lack of a tassel. Furthermore he was going to show his new best friend a trick only he and Benjie knew about. He'd show Tiffany how he could make his tassel go back and forth. Obviously these non-Christian men and boys didn't know what they were missing!

'That would be very nice, Mrs Kupper,' he said with a beatific smile.

Aunt Di visibly blanched – Uncle David by this stage had gotten back into the car and was slowly travelling back down the drive – 'It's *Auntie Di*, Jeremy dear,' she hissed. 'And it's Cowper, *not* Mrs Kupper! Wherever did *that* name spring from?' Despite a forced laugh the name in question was uttered with a startling vehemence.

'Oh, sorry Auntie Di'. Jeremy gave one of his most angelic smiles. 'I don't know *what* made me call you Mrs Kupper.' He turned to Tiffany. 'Have you got a swing?' he asked briskly, ignoring the still frowning woman.

The little girl gave a shrewd look followed by a peal of laughter. 'Bigger than yours!' she chortled. Taking him by the hand she glanced back at her still frowning mother. 'We'll be on the swing, Mummy,' she gaily cried. 'We'll come in for elevenses when Nina calls us!' Without further ado she pulled Jeremy along as she began to skip towards the side of the house. Once out of sight and out of hearing she came to an abrupt halt and, still holding Jeremy's hand, gave him a direct stare. 'Your uncle,' she said. 'When he got out of the car...'

'What?'

'He had *the* most enormous nose in his trousers!'

Diana Cowper stood looking at the corner to the house around which the two children had disappeared. 'Unpleasant little brat,' she muttered to herself. 'Kupper indeed!' She gave another shrug, thinking, but how on earth could he have come up with that?

Diana Cowper, nee Marsden, was herself not Jewish and had been surprised to find that the handsome, suave owner of the impressive jewellers shop in Bond Street, London was. As she later confided to a girlfriend, she shouldn't have been surprised, after all most of the people connected to that sort of trade 'were' – as she laughingly said – 'of that ilk.' Edward Cowper had turned his back completely on his Jewish roots and his marrying of the very Christian, very gentile Diana Marsden, had been one further step up the social ladder. The Marsdens epitomised the term 'solid middleclass', Diana's father being a successful stockbroker and her mother seen as a typical 'Sloane Ranger'. Diana, a plump, self-deprecating but jolly girl had been working with a small firm of interior decorators when the handsome jeweller had commissioned the company to redecorate his bachelor flat in the new Chelsea Harbour development. Edward, seeing the effusive, very 'jolly hockey sticks' girl as a definite asset to his social ambitions, had homed into her like a determined (and to Diana's unabashed delight) and very large guided missile. After a brief courtship – a flattered Diana had lost her virginity to the smooth

Edward on their second date and immediately found herself pregnant
– the two had married.

Edward, determined to live the life of an English gentleman had
bought 'The Manor' from a former client at a bargain price and as –
for what he deemed – a suitable weekend retreat, the Chelsea Harbour
flat having been forsaken for a grander establishment in Cadogan
Square. However, business ventures – and a rapacious mistress of
mixed race – saw him deserting London for increasing lengths of
time leading to Diana spending more and more time in the country
and less time in town. She had thrown herself into the everyday
happenings of the village with an energy that was almost comical.
Her friendship with Sybil Spiers was purely cosmetic, the lady of the
manor patronising the wife of the local vicar. The fact that she found
Sybil to be a neurotic bore was overlooked. Sybil fawned around her
as if she was minor royalty and this appealed to the blonde, buxom
Mrs Cowper. Again, Sybil was always willing to take upon herself the
most mundane of tasks. Looking after Tiffany was one of these and
now the Spiers boy had arrived on the scene the task would be easier
for, unbeknown to her arrogant philandering husband, Diana Cowper
was also having an affair.

Following in the footsteps of D.H. Lawrence's Lady Chatterley
she had become involved with Simon Cavell, a local farmer, whose
penchant for Rubens-inspired women was well-known. A wild
dalliance with Enid Smith, a local widow who ran a small antique
shop in the town, had confirmed his preference as had his romance
with Jane, the blonde barmaid at The Goose and Garter. Enid, a large,
voluptuous bleached blonde with a figure more Fern Britten than
Twiggy had taken over from Jane who, in her turn, was definitely
more mountain than maiden. The long suffering Mrs Cavell – to
everyone's astonishment – appeared as an almost anorexic figure who
had somehow managed not only to seduce and marry Simon but also
to present him with three healthy, strapping sons. Diana, not adverse
to spreading her 'charms' was also enjoying afternoons of violent,
sweaty sex with James, the middle son, a testosterone-infused lout
of eighteen. Neither father or son were aware that they were sharing
alternative afternoons with the buxom Mrs Cowper. Whereas it

had appeared slightly awkward having to ask her 'friend' to babysit whilst she, Diana, had to make endless trips up to London (Diana claimed to still be part of her former interior design business), the arrival of young Jeremy had been the proverbial blessing in disguise. The so-called trips to London became more frequent, London being a discreet country hotel for assignations with Cowper senior or the Holiday Inn in a more anonymous Brighton for Cavell junior. Diana's parents, initially shocked at the idea of their daughter marrying 'one of them' soon accepted the idea, claiming their new son-in-law had Italian blood and that the family jewellery business had its roots – as with the famous Bulgari family – in Italy. The Cowpers, when seen together, made a rather exotic couple, Edward with his dashing dark George Clooney-like looks and Diana, with her buxom, blonde Vanessa Feltz-like appearance. Needless to say the arrival of young Tiffany had done a lot to heal the rift between parents and daughter.

Giving her coiffed blonde head a shake, Diana Cowper had returned to her private study in the house where she clicked into her mobile. 'James' she said without introduction. 'Simply confirming Monday at noon.' Clicking off her phone she proceeded to idly shuffle through some papers on Edward's desk before buzzing through to Mrs Morgan, the cook, to inform her of one extra for lunch. 'Bloody cheek,' she said to a stuffed bird eyeing her beadily from its glass domed case (Edward collected stuffed birds and animals). 'Cheeky little shit calling me Kupper. Let him try it again and the little bastard won't know what's hit him!'

Meanwhile, Tiffany and Jeremy, ignoring the swing, had made their way to the pool house. Not only did 'The Manor' boast a swimming pool, outdoor tennis court and a stable block, there was also a mini-maze and a small lake. Jeremy, who had never seen such splendour, found it all quite overwhelming after the starkness and gloom of the vicarage.

Tiffany plumped herself down on a two seater cane settee, patting the brightly patterned cushion alongside her. 'Sit,' she commanded. Jeremy, immediately doing as he was told, gave the precocious little girl a wary look. 'What do you mean by my uncle having an enormous nose in his trousers?'

'Well he did,' said the little girl defiantly. 'You showed me your little nose the other day and when your uncle got out of the car he had an *enormous* one inside his trousers.'

'He didn't!'

'Did!'

'Didn't!'

'How do you know? You were still sitting in the car, silly. I *saw* it!' As if reading the disbelieving Jeremy's thoughts, she added, 'Can *you* make your nose bigger?'

'I er... don't know,' came Jeremy's hesitant reply. 'But I *do* know if *feels* as if it's getting bigger when I play slides or Benjie rubs!'

'Slides? Benjie rubs? What *do* you mean?' The small pink tongue sliding out in its moist concentration made up the little boy's mind for him.

'Look! I'll show you!' Quickly pulling down his trousers followed by his neat white underpants, Jeremy proudly displayed his – at this moment of time – extremely retroussé little penis. With a well-practised thumb and two fingers he tantalisingly pulled back the pink, crinkled foreskin to expose and even brighter pink marble-like head. 'Hello!' he cooed, waving his now definitely uncurling little projection at the completely riveted Tiffany. 'Goodbye!' he crooned, pulling the skin back over the head.

'Do it again!' demanded Tiffany. 'Or, better still, let *me* do it!'

Without giving Jeremy the chance to answer, she proceeded to briskly play 'helloes' and 'goodbyes' while Jeremy, always practical and never one to let a chance pass by, promptly lent forward and began sucking vigorously on Tiffany's bright pink glistening tongue sticking out in all its deepest concentrating glory.

A sudden spasm in his pee pee caused Jeremy to inadvertently bite down on the glorious, sweet tasting succulent treat. 'Ow!' came a muffled screech followed by a vicious retaliatory pinch.

'You bit me!' sulked Tiffany.

'You pinched me!' scowled Jeremy.

'Sorry,' said Tiffany.

'Me too,' said Jeremy.

'Hello!' said Tiffany just before she allowed Jeremy to shut her up again in his most delicious way.

A still uptight Diana Cowper looked on somewhat mystified at the two semi-hysterical children continued shrieking 'goodbye' to each other as Jeremy was chauffeured away in the family Mercedes.

The phone call came two days later. Once again Jeremy was to be sent to purdah, Tiffany having ridiculed her apoplectic father for not being able to play 'helloes' and 'goodbyes.'

'Jeremy told me so,' she had informed her outraged parents having announced that she too, wanted to be like Miriam Finkelstein whom Edward had scathingly dubbed 'a Jewish princess.'

'Jeremy says Daddy's a Jew because he's had his willy hat cut off which means I can be a Jewish jewel as well as a princess! But it also means Daddy can't play "helloes!"' she added once more with wicked satisfaction.'

'Explain these "helloes" and "goodbyes?"' expostulated her red-faced father.

Eyeing her visibly shocked mother Tiffany had sweetly explained. 'Mummy, I *can't* make Daddy's willy say "hello" 'cos you'd be cross and, unless Jeremy is telling fibs, Daddy – as I've already said (there was a strong hint of impatience here) – Daddy can't play *anyway,* because he hasn't got a willy hat!'

'I suggest you get onto that Spiers woman, *tout de suite,* and tell her that her nephew is never to set foot in this house nor speak to our daughter again! In fact, ban the bloody lot of them, that idiotic dog collar and his social climbing wife!' It had taken all of Edward's innate control to stop himself from shaking his little daughter who, for some reason known only to herself, had suddenly stuck out her tongue at *him.*

'Oh Jeremy, what *have* you done?' croaked Auntie Sybil, slumping down in a quivering heap alongside the kitchen table, the portable phone still in her hand, Diana Cowper, her *greatest* friend, having just told her coolly and without any explanation that there would be no further connection between the two families.

'Nothing, Auntie Sybil,' came the injured reply. 'I only asked Auntie Di why she called herself Mrs Cowper after Uncle David had told me their real name is Kupper and Uncle Edward is not a Gentile but a Jew!'

Jeremy's only reaction at the sight of his aunt crashing to the floor was to walk over to the cookie jar and help himself to a piece of shortbread.

The following altercation between his uncle and aunt was spectacular. Again Jeremy was grounded for a week and again his play station made out of bounds. That night the scowling boy removed the bottle of bleach from where he had hidden it at the bottom of his toy cupboard.

CHAPTER 2

'Terrible about what 'appended to that poor Mrs Spiers, the vicar's wife.' Said Mrs Morgan, the Cowper's cook with a certain amount of relish.

'What?' said Diana disinterestedly, her mind focussing on the *placement* for the dinner party they were holding that evening and *not* the incessant chatter of her always gossipy cook.

''Orrible! Quite 'orrible!' said Mrs Morgan, more loudly this time. 'And that poor little tyke, having to find her and all!'

'What *are* you going on about, Mrs Morgan?' said Diana irritably. '*What* has happened to Mrs Spiers and what on earth *ghastly* enough could have happened to upset that "poor little tyke?"' (Diana, still reeling from Tiffany's denouement had thought for a moment the cook had said *kike*!).

Having got her audience, Mrs Morgan put down the apple corer (in an act of defiance Diana had ordered a pork shoulder roast with apple stuffing as the main course for the evening's dinner) and folding her brawny arms, began. 'Well...'

It took several 'please, Mrs Morgan, I haven't go all day!' frustrated cries before Diana got the full story. Poor Sybil Spiers, as part of her nightly routine, had, on this particular occasion, asked little Jeremy to pour out her usual glass of milk, and he, poor little soul, had mistakenly poured her a glass of liquid bleach instead! How the mix up could have happened, nobody quite knew, but the inconsolable Jeremy had insisted Auntie Sybil had pointed to the bottle (incapable of pouring the drink herself she had apparently set the milk down next to the bottle of bleach) which she insisted was the drink she wished for instead. Jeremy had later tearfully confided that he *knew* it wasn't milk but then, as Auntie Sybil was always drinking a lot 'of the other!' so he had given it little thought.

The damage was further aggravated by the 'little dear' unknowingly giving his choking, screaming aunt even *more* of the same liquid *after* she had collapsed onto the floor, *thinking it may help her*! Here Mrs Morgan could not resist the bon mot to end all bons mots. 'Poor laddie also told us that Auntie Sybil now seemed to be always falling onto the floor!'

'Where is she?' gasped Diana, the *placement* momentarily forgotten.

'In intensive care at the local hospital!' came the smug reply.

According to Mrs Morgan's friend, Dora, who helped out at the vicarage, Mrs Spiers hadn't been 'quite herself' for a few weeks and had 'been drinking…a lot!'

'Is the young boy alright?'

'Distraught, Mrs C. Quite, quite distraught! Thank goodness he's got the Reverend to turn to!'

Had Mrs Morgan been more accurate, it was the quite other way round with the Very Reverend David Spiers turning to a very receptive Jeremy. Quite by accident, on the night following the unfortunate incident, after which a still inconsolable Jeremy had whisperingly asked Uncle David if he could sleep in the big bed with him, what begun as a cuddle had ended as a frantic game of hellos and goodbyes with Uncle David winning by a very long and very wet shot!

Auntie Sybil, not being a survivor and, having been duly blessed by Uncle David, had lingered for only a few more days before going on to join her deceased kith and kin in the great bleached yonder. Jeremy never returned to his own, claustrophobic room.

Diana Cowper, having suffered a minor attack of guilt (she'd nearly confessed to her banning of 'that Spiers lot' to the burly Simon Cavell after one turbulent afternoon of wild sex in their sweaty four poster bed in the usual country hidey-hole) finally capitulated to Tiffany's continual, verging on the truculent, demands to see Jeremy.

A wiser Jeremy not only allowed Tiffany to play 'helloes', but he also introduced her to the pleasures of 'pooh fingers.' As yet unable to spurt like Uncle David he had been encouraged to push his bunched fingers and hand up into his uncle's hot, receptive 'pooh hole' with Uncle David reciprocating by pushing a large, hairy finger up his!

'Pooh fingers' with Tiffany saw them both sticking their tiny fingers up each other's rears, pulling them out, sniffing them and chortling with fiendish glee, 'Pooh fingers!'

It was not long before Tiffany had the benefit of the game being played both fore and aft. And it was not long after this that Uncle David hoarsely suggested that instead of his finger, maybe he could try something else? Jeremy was hooked.

A bewildered Tiffany suddenly found herself 'No Longer Wanted on The Voyage.' Jeremy to his zealous delight had suddenly discovered the secret of true power, not that of a particularly vicious or unpleasant misdeed, but that of absolute, mental control over another; Uncle David now belonging to him and him completely. The man's obsession with his nephew saw him becoming more and more under the young boy's power, so much so that the confused and mentally tortured man finally forced himself to do what he dreaded most and send his blond angel off to a distant boarding school. While Uncle David pined for his lost now thirteen year old Ganymede, the 'mythological' boy in question was to rise 'like a Phoenix' from the imaginary vicarage ashes.

Rayner's School for Boys, set in a mountainous region of northern Scotland had been highly recommended to David Spiers, not only as a set of learning but as one of the best all round schools in the country. Claiming the same illustrious status as its rival Gordonstoun whose most famous pupil had been Prince Charles, David had been heard to jocularly quip, 'can you think of a better reason for me selecting the alternative?!' In normal circumstances the school, with its astronomical fees of some £23,000 per annum, would have way beyond the Very Reverend's meagre pocket but, thanks to monies left by his brother for the sole purpose of his son's education, Jeremy was able to attend.

Caught up in a new world of excitement and wealth, Jeremy – benefitting from a substantial inheritance – had been allotted a small but adequate allowance dating from his thirteenth birthday. As a result his earlier years as a schoolboy at the local primary along with the fawning devotion of his uncle were soon forgotten. The fledgling teenager, armed with his looks, intelligence and finely honed inner cunning (such power is a lethal drug) soon became one of the most popular – and ruthless – pupils the school had the pleasure to welcome to its bleak but beneficial environment.

At the end of his first year he had ruthlessly wooed and won over the head of his house and, in his best clandestine manner, gone on to seduce two of his teachers. This heady game of cat and mouse saw him an expert and, when the time came for him to leave, the name Jeremy Spiers was one whispered in almost hallowed and certainly reverend tones!

David, by this stage and much to the chagrin of his parishioners, had become an embittered, vindictive elderly man whose Sunday sermons seemed to be more of a rant against the injustices of society towards him than the welfare of his flock. The eagerly awaited holidays when Jeremy deigned to make a brief appearance at the vicarage (mostly he was invited away to some exotic getaway as a guest of another besotted pupil) saw Jeremy at his best. Forget the pulling of the heads of fledgling chicks; forget boiling vacuous gold fish; forget cremating your family and poisoning your aunt; the slow, satisfying and complete psychological destruction of his uncle was to be one of his penultimate triumphs.

'Good morning, my dear,' said the vicar tremulously. 'Sleep well?'

A blond, tousled Jeremy, now aged sixteen, gave the nervous, elderly man a cold, blue-eyed laser-like stare. 'Yes, but no thanks to you! Haven't I told you *not* to disturb me on the first night of my return as I simply have to relocate myself mentally for this shit heap you expect me to call home? I'll sleep with you *tonight* if the mood takes me but until then, I suggest you stick to my old bed room!'

'Yes, Jeremy,' said his uncle in a suitably chastened whisper.

'Coffee!' Jeremy demanded, sitting himself down and letting out a prolonged fart. 'Ah, air freshener!' he added glibly. 'Something this heap sorely needs.'

'Yes, Jeremy,' repeated the broken man, pouring the coffee with a shaking hand.

'Tell you what,' added his nephew, taking a small sip from the steaming mug, 'let's play a new game!'

'Yes?' said the meek man, always eager to please.

'As you seem *so* determined to play the subservient house frau may I suggest you do so one hundred percent! Tomorrow I'd like to see you in one of my dear, deceased aunt's housecoats or perhaps she only had one? Whatever, house coat and her slippers, perhaps?' Looking at his uncle's receding hairline he gave a cruel giggle. 'Just as well you're a balding old sod otherwise I would have demanded curlers!'

'Would you like me to change for you now?' quavered the old man, always willing to please the blond, strapping god who seemed hell bent on his destruction.

Jeremy eyed the rheumy-eyed man looking across at him with open devotion from over the sparsely laid breakfast table. 'Why not, *Sybil*!' said his nephew.

Fifteen minutes later Jeremy fucked the bucking, weeping, writhing groaning *Sybil,* as he lay spread-eagled in glorious submission on top of the kitchen table, his former wife's nightdress (there was no housecoat) hoisted up above his pale, skinny shanks to expose a flaccid receptive arse.

'I suppose you could say I've just given you my own version of a *well-cum* home present,' smirked Jeremy as he drew his now prestigious length from his whimpering uncle. Jeremy, it must be said, having reached the age of sixteen was a definite, living proof of the ancient proverb, '*Mighty oaks from little acorns grow.*'

Later, sitting alone in the empty kitchen – Uncle David having gone to douche and prepare himself for another day of resolution – Jeremy was busily planning his next holiday treat.

'Now I've dealt with you for the time being, your desperate old, sad handmaiden of your Christian God, it's onward and decidedly untoward with the next festering fury on my list! Why not a visit by a rabid rabbi to our dear Mr and Mrs "call me Cowper" Kupper? Oh yes, dear Kuppers, I do think it's definitely time for *your* come-*uppance*!'

Having lost all contact with Tiffany, Jeremy still bore an enormous grudge against her parents, her mother in particular. Unable to 'deal with the counterfeit cunt and her counterfeit cut cunt of a husband' – his special name for the Cowpers – while still attending boarding school, Jeremy had bided his time. On this occasion his revenge was to be a very cold dish but one the Cooper's would have given every bit of jewellery in Edward's proud and much cherished possession to avoid.

'Tone? Jer! How are you, my friend?'

'Jer? Great to hear you man! When did you get back?'

'Yesterday.'

'You buying?'

'If you're still selling!'

'Is the Pope still catholic? Usual place say six?'

'You're on. And Tone, I've got another small job for you, a bit of very nasty wham, bam and no thank you mam!'

'Sounds cool! See you at six and we can talk about it then.'

Tone, alias Franchot Seaton (the Tone being a nickname based on the Christian name of fifties actor Franchot Tone, a man for whom Tone's mother, Violet, a black single mother with a penchant for shoplifting, held a particular fondness), had been a contact through another school friend. While his mother thieved, Tone dealt. 'Toned and Stoned,' was the ruthless black man's mantra and his dealing with Jeremy and his school friends was second to none.

It was by sheer coincidence that the dealer – now in his early twenties – should have been based in Jeremy's home town. Tone's second mantra, 'Deals on Wheels,' followed his propensity for travelling the length and breadth of the country 'for the sake of his art!'

His visits to the nearby small town which served Rayner's School were made known well in advance and clandestine meetings in one of the town's more dubious coffee bars were enthusiastically attended. Jeremy had been introduced to the delights of *Charlie* but was not prepared to indulge in anything more habit forming or dangerous. Franchot, as he referred to himself in his more serious moments, respected his young client for this, subsequently never pushing a different sale.

In one of the few moments when the two had sat themselves down and had a serious heart-to-heart in the Flamingo Coffee Bar, Jeremy, with less candour than usual had found himself pouring out all his pent up frustrations and inward anger to the sympathetic black man.

Sitting back and staring at the sullen young man sitting in front of him, Tone had softly said, 'Yer gay, ain't you, Jer?'

Jeremy, having indulged in mutual masturbation and the occasional anal sex (plus either wanking off his uncle or, as a whimpering David now demanded more and more, actually fucking him) hadn't actually given the question much thought.

'Why?' he casually asked. 'Are you?'

'Yeah, now and then when I feel like it,' said Tone, without hesitation, 'Yeah, call me half and half and what's more, I wouldn't mind fucking you if you'll let me!'

'What's in it for me?' added Jeremy slyly.

'A couple of grams, maybe!'

'You're on,' said the young man with a laugh, adding, 'It'll be interesting to see if what they say about you black guys is true or not!'

'Oh, in my case it's true. Being fucked by the Big Tone is guaranteed to *make you moan*!'

Franchot shared a maisonette with his light-fingered mother in one of less distinguished areas of the town. To Jeremy's pleasant surprise the interior of the two bedroom, double floored flat was done out with considerable style and flair – 'neat and sweet' is how his host described it – with a mixture of modern, comfortable seating units, cube tables and several large, colourful wall canvasses which, to Jeremy's disbelief, had been painted by the non-uniform dealer. However, dominating the main room was a vast collection of dolls sitting on almost every available surface and inside a series of brightly-coloured wooden shelves. 'Put it down to me for the modern art and Violet for the voodoo!' quipped the grinning son.

As soon as they had entered through the heavily enforced front door (Tone having had to undo at least six mortice locks and saying, with a grunt of satisfaction, 'maybe the old girl's not back in yet!') Tone had grabbed a startled Jeremy by the crotch. 'Nice,' he said, kneading Jeremy's immediate receptive hardening, 'very nice. Now let's get it out and have a look at what you, young Jer, have to offer!'

'What about you?' came the gasped reply as Tone quickly unzipped Jeremy's fly, thus releasing his rampant cock which sprang up reminiscent of an energetic Jack-in-the-box.

'You deal with it,' murmured Tone before pushing his mouth onto Jeremy's and forcing an enormous, thick, spittle-covered tongue in between the boy's now parted teeth. Meanwhile the visibly excited black man, quickly wiping his fore and index fingers through the copious saliva drooling down between their chins, proceeded to push them both slowly and determinedly up into Jeremy's hot, moist arsehole.

'Ow!' Expostulated Jeremy. 'Ow! Ouch! Easy, *easy* Tone…'

'And that's for starters!' mumbled his host through a tangle of tongues.

Stumbling and hopping the two managed to kick off their shoes (in Tone's case, trainers), trousers and underpants before falling onto one of the large, soft sofas.

'Get a load of this, Jer!' gasped Tone, waving his enormous black, heavily veined, purple-domed swollen cock in front of the wide-eyed teenager. 'Tell me seeing's not believing!'

'Fuck, Tone,' spluttered Jeremy. 'That's not a cock, it's a fucking stick of dynamite!'

'And about to explode up your arse!' Without hesitation, the muscular black man threw Jeremy onto his back, spat vigorously into a large pink palm and, hefting the young man's lithe, muscular legs up onto his broad shoulders, deeply impaled him with one sword-like thrust.

'*Ow, ow, ow!*' squawked Jeremy.

'Ow? Ow? Or how, how?' With a cry of pure primal delight Tone began to pump, piston-like into Jeremy's rapidly opening and closing warm, wet, squelching greedy hole. 'Howzat, hey?' panted Tone, his pace quickening; his viciously stabbing cock no more than a blur. '*Howzat?*'

'Jesus! I'm coming! I'm coming!' yelled Jeremy, his legs starting to thresh in Tone's vice-like arms.

'Aaaaah!' howled a rutting, twisting, bouncing Tone. 'Aaaaah!' he cried again as Jeremy jettisoned an arc of hot, pearlescent globules onto his sweat drenched, heaving chest. With a final triumphant shout he juddered and shuddered, climaxing deep down inside the bucking, receptive Jeremy.

'Jesus!' said Jeremy for the umpteenth time as they lay slumped in sweat-drenched lassitude side by side. 'Jesus, Tone. I came like that without even touching myself!' the disbelief in his voice saying it all.

'It's that old black magic along with a bit of Violet's voodoo dolls!' laughed Tone, his white teeth sparkling in his sweat streaked black face.

'Did I hear my name used in vain?' came a querulous voice from the top of the stairs.

'Fuck it, Mama!' yelped Tone, jumping to his feet, his long, thick cum-enhanced cock still semi-erect. 'Don't you know surprising a black boy like that can make him go white with fright?'

'Well, before you do a Michael Jackson, son, your whiter than white, innocent, pure-as-the-driven snow Violet wouldn't say no to a large rum and Coke with *lots* of ice! Listening to you two *hard* at it has given me quite a thirst!'

'I thought you said your ma was *out*?' hissed Jeremy, quickly reaching for his scattered clothes.

'So I did,' said Tone, making his way, stark naked, towards the neat kitchenette. 'But I can't be right *all* the time, now, can I?'

Violet, her rum and Coke duly delivered, shouted down a further instruction before slamming her bedroom door shut. 'Now you two make sure there be no slimy smears on my sofa down there! Give me ten minutes or so and I'll be down for another rum and C. You can then introduce me to that very noisy friend of yours!' There was a profound silence followed by a distinct chuckle and giggly 'Howzat?'

'Well, we've well and truly discussed the first point raised by you, Jer (here Tone gave his bulging crotch a pat), so, what's the other?' he demanded, the two now dressed and facing each other, an iced rum and Coke held in their respective hands.

'A couple called Cowper.' Jeremy took a deep swallow of his drink. 'Let me explain. Ten minutes later (Violet had still to make her descent) Tone, eyeing the anxious Jeremy now sitting forward on the edge of his seat, his drink forgotten, could only say admiringly, 'It's the bollocks, Jer! It's bloody fucking brilliant! How the *fuck* did you ever get to dream up that sort of shit?'

CHAPTER 3

'Mrs Cowper? Good evening. You may not remember me, Jeremy. Jeremy Spiers, Sybil Spiers's nephew.'

'Oh!' There was a moment's silence. 'Yes, of course I remember you!' said the plummy voice followed by a further distinctive pause, then an imperious, 'Are you still there?'

'Oh yes, Mrs Cowper,' came the soft, silky reply, 'I'm most definitely still here!' After another moment's uncomfortable silence he added, 'Is Tiffany around?'

'Tiffany? Oh...' – here the woman's relief was obvious – 'no, I'm afraid not. She's away at finishing school in Switzerland.'

'Ah, the land of the cuckoo cocks,' said Jeremy knowingly.

'What?' Diana Cowper shook her perfectly coiffed head irritably. She could have *sworn* she'd heard cock instead of clock, exactly like the time with tyke and kike! This dreadful young man seemed to always have the most extraordinary effect on her hearing.

'That's a pity,' continued Jeremy, blithely ignoring her question, but with a distinct hint of sarcasm in his voice. 'It would have been fun to say hello again! So much nicer a hello than a goodbye, isn't it? If you catch my drift!' Diana's quick intake of breath was audible over the phone. 'Hey, Mrs *Cowper,* wouldn't it be fun to meet for old time's sake? I'd love to pop round!'

'We're out this evening!' came the immediate response.

'Pity,' murmured Jeremy, It's the only evening I've got free before I leave for the continent tomorrow.'

'Oh?' The sound was one of relief. 'Somewhere nice?'

'Switzerland!' said Jeremy, clicking off his mobile before Mrs Cowper had a chance to respond.

'We're on,' he said, turning to Tone. 'Tonight. They're in for the evening – she made that little fact so fucking obvious!'

'Are we expecting someone?' Edward Cowper looked up at his wife sitting opposite him in the elegant, book-lined study. 'I thought I heard the front door bell.'

'No, nobody,' said his wife, barely glancing up from the latest best-seller by Robin Anderson on her lap. 'Besides, you *know* Thursday is the staff's night off and we never, ever entertain on a Thursday! We haven't done so for the past twenty years!'

'OK! OK!' said her husband placatingly, 'Keep your Janet Reger's on! Damn. There it goes again! I'd better go and take a look. Probably some idiot wanting road directions. I'll slaughter Parson's for leaving those bloody gates open!'

'Don't swear, dear. It isn't nice,' murmured Diana, going back to her novel. 'And yes dear, *do* go and answer the main front door... vent some of your vicious spleen on some innocent member of the public!'

'Oh, piss off!' muttered Edward, rising to his feet.

'I heard that,' said his wife sweetly, turning a page.

'Yes?' Edward looks askance at the two men, one white, one black, standing under the front portico.

'Yes?' he demanded again, this time his voice less assured. Like most whites he was innately uncomfortable in the presence of blacks and to see one with an obvious white soulmate sent an involuntary shiver down his spine.

'Mr Kupper!' said Jeremy, giving his most disarming smile. 'It's Jeremy, Jeremy Spiers, Tiffany's childhood friend! We used to *play* together! Surely you must remember me?'

'You've grown,' responded Edward curtly. 'My wife told you our daughter's not here (Diana had briefly relayed the call to her husband earlier) so, what do you want?'

'A drink would be nice, Mr Kupper oh, how *rude* of me! Please let me introduce my business associate, Mr Franchot Seaton. Franchott can be one mean, nasty fucker if wanting to meet with your worst nightmare is ever on your agenda; *can't* you, Franchot?'

A decidedly nervous Edward held out a tentative hand which Tone grasped and pumped with exaggerated enthusiasm. 'Cool to meet you Mr Kupper!' he beamed, showing a gleaming row of teeth.

'Cowper,' said Edward Kupper automatically.

'*Kupper*!' said Jeremy firmly, making as if to push his way past the startled man, but then changing his mind. 'And where's dear Auntie "I'm fucking half the local farmhands" Di?' Noting the genuine look of puzzlement on Edward's face, Jeremy shook his blond head, making a soft tut tutting. 'Oh, poor Uncle Edward, didn't you know? Big Simon Clavell and sonny boy James, both of whom – according to pub rumour – are impressively endowed as well as being known as the local barnyard studs, are also known to have been regularly fucking your bovine wife!' Tut tutting again he turned from an ashen-faced Edward back to Tone. 'You see Franchot, it's always the cuckold husband who's last to know.'

'Get out!' roared Edward, his nervousness turning to fury. 'Get out this instant before I call the police!'

'Get out, Uncle Edward? Get out before you call the police? Oh, no no no *no*! You've got it all wrong. We're here to get *in* and the police coming your way is in the form of Franchot's own frightening big black truncheon!'

Grabbing a startled Edward he spun him round to face back into the grand hallway. 'OK MacDuff, lead us on to the much furrowed Mrs Kupper!'

'Take your filthy hands off me, immediately!' shouted Edward, inwardly praying that Diana, perhaps perplexed by his long absence, would have had the nuance to check on him and, witnessing the confrontation, have locked herself in the study and was now phoning the police.

Jeremy's reaction to the man's demands was a hissed, 'Fuck you, Kupper!' followed by slamming his fist onto the man's surgically enhanced nose. 'I said, lead on! Not fight back!'

'Edward?' Diana's anxious voice (she had been unable to ignore the raised voices) came floating across the wide, tiled hallway.

'Ah, I do believe "Our Lady of the Charitable Cunt" may be in the study!' Grabbing Edward's left arm he twisted it viciously up behind his back, gesturing Tone to do the same with the right.

'*Edward*!' Diana's voice was now more frightened than querulous.

'Here, darlin'! Here!' cooed Tone in his best Caribbean accent. 'Da big black bogey man is heah!'

'Oh my God!' Diana gave a small, high pitched scream. Making her way nervously into the hallway she suddenly stopped. 'Jeremy! Yes, I know it's you! What on *earth* do you think you're doing? Leave my husband alone, *at once*!'

'Leave your husband alone, at once?' Jeremy's mouth twisted into an unpleasant smirk. 'But, my dear, darling Auntie Di, we haven't even *started* on him yet!'

Giving out a high pitched wail the woman made a dash for the study door but Tone was the faster of the two. Letting go of Edward's arm he bounded across the hallway, grabbing the terrified woman as she valiantly tried to shut herself in.

'*Naughty* Di!' Tone cried. 'Naughty, naughty Di!' Giving the shrieking woman a resounding slap across her face, he grabbed her before she could fall, frogmarching her back into the study. In perfect synchronisation both he and Jeremy threw the helpless couple down onto one of the chesterfield-style sofas.

'What is it you want?' gasped Edward nasally, his obviously broken nose still streaming blood. 'What the *hell* do you want?'

'Want? Want? Surely that's your little game, Mr Kupper? Always wanting! We don't want anything *material* from you, Jew! All we *want* is to play some very nasty games seriously, *seriously* involving the two of you!' Jeremy pointed to the rucksack Tone was wearing. 'Rope, please Tone. Let's truss up our counterfeiters and then, *let the fun begin!*'

Diana began to scream in sheer, undiluted terror, only to be silenced by a second vicious slap from Tone. 'Shut-the-fuck-up-Auntie-Di!' hissed the now obviously aroused black man. 'Just-shut-the-fuck-up!' He turned to a broadly smiling Jeremy. 'Phase one, Jer?'

'As planned Tone. Let the rabbi-ing begin!'

Diana, as with Edward, their arms bound securely across their chests (Diana had let out a further scream but one of outrage as Tone viciously squeezed one breast) was now picked up by Tone who dumped her unceremoniously in the swivel chair behind the large desk. 'Best seat in the stalls,' he chuckled. Adding insult to injury he grabbed one of the many stuffed ducks sitting on one of the bookshelves, dumping this equally as unceremoniously on the startled woman's head. 'Party hat for party time!' he chuckled again.

'Fuck you!' spat Diana, shaking the bird from its unexpected perch.

'Oh no, Auntie Di! It's the other way round!' Tone gave a flash of his brilliant teeth. 'We're both going to be fucking *you!*'

The woman emitted a small, terrified whimper.

'OK, Franchot! Let's deal with Mr Kupper.' Said Jeremy, his voice briskly efficient. Bending over the sullen man he quickly undid his belt before shucking down his trousers and boxer shorts to reveal his thick, flaccid circumcised penis.

'We're going to have to play *Reverses,* Uncle David, as opposed to "helloes" and "goodbyes," because, as you know you don't have a party hat to tip for "hello" and drop again for "goodbye!"'

'*Reverses,* Jer?' said Tone, tuning into their previously rehearsed banter.

'Yes, Tone,' beamed Jeremy. '*Reverses.* As Uncle David – er, Mr Kupper, is a Jewish gentleman who, for some reason known only to himself, insists on being a Gentile gent, namely Mr Cowper! And, as you and I are *so* accommodating, his most fervent wish is now to be granted!'

'And how do we turn Mr Kupper into Mr Cowper, Jer?'

'Why, that's where *you* come in, *Rabbi* Tone. You have to *un*-circumcise him!'

'But Jer, like Houston, we have a problem.'

'Oh?'

'How do you un-circumcise someone who is already circumcised?'

'Simple, Rabbi Tone. You cut away all the bald evidence back to its base where there is plenty of the original skin!'

'Ah, so original skin to look like foreskin!'

'Exactly! You will have, in a manner of sorts, put him back the way he was! Kupper now a kosher Cowper!'

Edward and Diana began to simultaneously scream.

Ignoring the hysterical, struggling couple, Jeremy continued, 'Do you have your circumcision special, Rabbi Tone?'

'Indeed I do, Jer, somewhere in my bag of tricks.' He glanced at the shrieking couple. 'Honestly Jer, how will they expect me to concentrate with all that noise.'

'I agree Tone! Ah! Look, ready gags galore!' With a quick movement Jeremy picked up Diana's discarded stuffed duck and, ripping off the wings, stuffed these into the noisy, open mouths. 'Reminds me of my fledglings, Tone?'

'What?'

'Later, Rabbi Tone. Later.'

Tone, having shuffled theatrically inside his satchel, drew out a gleaming scalpel. 'Here we are!' he cried. 'The local chemist's best! Disposable too!'

'Only one, Rabbi T?'

'Oh no, Jer, I'm *well* prepared!'

Edward, his eyes bulging and his head tossing wildly was now making wild, muffled grunts through the feathers protruding from his mouth.

'Right,' said Jeremy. 'Let the rabbi-ing begin!'

Leaning forward he grabbed Edward's cock by the base, stretching it as far as he could, allowing for the fully exposed, gleaming, bulbous head to point up at Tone who, holding the rounded head in the palm of his hand, simply severed it from its stem.

Edward vomited out the duck's wing, his hoarse shrieks of pain reverberating round the room. Without a pause Tone bent down and, picking up the pink, bloody ball from the carpet and jammed it into the man's mouth. 'Chew on that, Eddie boy!' he snarled. Turning back to Jeremy who by now was literally doubled up with laughter, he asked, dead pan. 'What next, Jer, now that Rabbi Tone's completed his little task?'

'His jewels, Tone. After all, he's a jeweller and must expect to be robbed of his jewels, sooner or later!'

Within seconds Edward had been castrated.

'More gag fodder!' chortled Tone, stuffing the bloody sac in the wake of the head to his cock.

'He's obviously got a good eye for business!' camped Jeremy.

'Nooooo!' screamed Diana, who like, Edward, had managed to spit out the duck's wing. 'For God's sake, Jeremy! I beg you!'

'It's rude to spit!' said Jeremy crossing over to the nigh-on-demented woman and jamming the regurgitated wing back crudely into her gaping mouth.

Without hesitation Tone took out Edward's right eyeball.

'Don't *Passover* the leftover!' quipped Jeremy.

Without flinching, Tone deftly took out Edward's left eyeball.

'Damn!' muttered Jeremy. 'Too soon Tone!'

'Why?'

'Because now the bastard can't see what we're about to do to his wife, that's why!' said Jeremy, playing at being petulant.

'But his ears are OK!' laughed Tone.

'Hear! Hear!' chortled Jeremy.

With a coughing, spluttering sound Edward choked out the bloody contents from his mouth and throat. 'Sick bastards...' he managed to croak, the sound racked with the deepest sorrow and pain.

'The larynx?' questioned Jeremy. 'Christ! The noise from these two!'

'A bit too technical, even for a genius like me,' mused Tone. 'Better skip that but I could easily manage a finger or two!'

'From money fingers to butter fingers!' camped Jeremy. 'Off you go or, shouldn't that be, *off they come?*' the play on words resulting in peals of laughter.

Edward passed out on the removal of his eighth finger.

'Keep the fingers for later,' insisted Jeremy. 'I've a brilliant idea!'

After they'd both simultaneously fucked a sobbing, quietly moaning Diana, Tone from the front and Jeremy from the rear, the woman was then subjected to one final, grotesque humiliation. Three of her husband's fingers were rammed up deeply into her arse and three similarly embedded inside her cunt. Diana's last memory was being forced to eat a finger supper comprising of Edward's index fingers which Tone, with the help of a paper weight, had mashed into a splintery pulp.

'Enjoy your last supper, Aunite Di,' cooed Jeremy, massaging the finger supper down Diana's gagging throat. 'And as a good *Jewish* girl you'll be happy to know that after two circumcisions – the un-circumcision was a sick joke – your husband's fingers are one hundred and *ten* per cent kosher!'

Several minutes later Tone deftly slit Edward's throat. 'I *told* you, Jer, I would never have managed that larynx job!' he camped as Edward's blood jettisoned out over the sofa.

'Nobody's perfect, not even you, Tone!' came the quick reply. Glancing at the two corpses, Jeremy nodded towards the obvious erection in Tone's jeans. 'I see, like me, this has really turned you on and so, my friend, what do you say, big Tone, to making young Jer here groan *and* moan?'

'Oh my, oh my!' laughed a stark naked Tone a few moments later, liberally lubricating his huge, rampant erection. Scooping up another handful from its unexpected source, he couldn't resist adding, 'Forget your Chrisco, forget your KY! With Uncle Eddie's voodoo blood on my dick we're both going to fly!'

The complete gutting of 'The Manor' by a mysterious fire dominated the local papers for a day or two, allowing Mrs Morgan her fifteen minutes of fame as *The One Who Could Have Been There*. After several more 'blood donations' – courtesy of Edward – Jeremy and Tone had been meticulous in covering their tracks. It took several days before the bodies of the popular jeweller and his wife were discovered, side by side, on what appeared to be the remains of a sofa. ('Always so close,' Mrs Morgan had sniffed, 'Must 'ave died in each others arms!'). The delay in finding the bodies had been due to enormous amount of rubble caused by the whole building collapsing. The cause of the devastating fire was eventually put down to an electrical fault cleverly staged by the ever-accommodating Tone.

CHAPTER 4

EIGHTEEN MONTHS LATER:

'Tone, I've been thinking.'

'Oh no, no more personal vendettas, please! I'm still looking over my shoulder because of the last one!'

Jeremy gave a small laugh. 'No, no more vendettas; more about you and me.'

'Oh no... that's even worse! Please, *please* tell me you're not about to ask me to go through some civil ceremony shit with you!'

'I don't believe in mixed-race children!'

'Fuck you!'

'Yes please – but later!' Jeremy gave another laugh. 'Now, my friend, please listen. Try and be serious for a moment.'

The two were lying side by side on their individual sun loungers alongside the azure blue pool set in the colourful gardens surrounding famous Phonecia Hotel on the Mediterranean island of Malta.

'My "delayed thank you treat" for helping me with operation *Scupper the Kupper* or operation *Foreskin Formidable*!' as Jeremy had so succinctly put it.

'If you'd stop looking at my python-like dick trying to get comfortable in these Speedos,' came the laconic reply, 'then you'd see I'm all ears!'

'How much money have you got stashed away?'

'Hey! Hey!' The unexpectedness of the question saw Tone sitting upright, his eyes flashing angrily. 'Just don't go there, Jer!'

'Oh, shut up, Tone! I'm not suddenly going to turn rent boy to your bent boy! No, I'm serious, listen.' Beckoning a nearby waiter he ordered a bottle of the local Chardonnay and, once the wine was poured, continued. 'I've been thinking – and don't even think of starting to laugh! I've finished with school and the thought of going onto a university just for the sake of something to do, has no appeal what-so-ever. Thanks to a small allowance which came into fruition last year I've been able to faff around doing more-or-less what I please but I really now want something more tangible to hook on to.'

'Take up bullshit writing for starters!'

'Shut the fuck off and listen!' Jeremy took another long sip of his drink. 'That was last year's little treat. I've now been working out how much I come into on my next birthday. Thank Christ my father wasn't one of those *twenty one today* arseholes and I get the first real, hard dollop from both his and dear mama's insurances *plus, plus* and more *plus* in a few month's time. A cool half a million…'

'Jesus Christ! If you can fix it, I'll go through the fucking ceremony this afternoon! No! Can't we go somewhere *now*?'

'Don't be a total arsehole all your tinted, tainted life, *arsehole*! And that's not just with your big white colonial master here!'

'*Yebo* bwana! Sorry bwana!' camped Tone, more Robert de Niro than Rudyard Kipling.

'That's better! Much, much better!' smiled Jeremy. He gave Tone a small pat on a large, glistening ebony-hued thigh. 'Apart from your wheeling and dealing, what else do you *really* enjoy?'

'Well, bwana, with all due respect it ain't really fucking you! Or maybe that's all now changed with half a million in the bank as a lubricant!'

'I said *be serious*!'

'I thought fucking you *was* serious!'

Jeremy, choosing to ignore Tone's chuckled remark, carried on. 'You enjoy painting, don't you? And not only do you enjoy it, you're also bloody good at it!'

'You're getting there bride-about-to-be! Half a million and now bullshit flattery about my painting, what next? You going to start introducing me as the first black Jackson Pollock?'

'Not quite! I was thinking more of an exhibition.'

'Exhibition?'

'Yes an exhibition. And *not* featuring the *first black bollock Pollack,* but the one and only Franchot Seaton!'

'You don't have to take up writing bullshit. You spew it out so well!'

Jeremy, ignoring the comment, continued. 'As I said, I really want something more tangible to hook on to. A purpose.'

'Oh shit,' groaned Tone. 'Bring on the violins – no, better still' – he beckoned for the waiter – 'another bottle of wine. I think we're both going to need it!'

'So I've decided, I want to open an art gallery, a bona fide art gallery…'

'I like the *boner* part!'

'For fuck's sake Tone! Listen! A *serious* gallery catering for unknown, up-and-coming – don't you *dare* – artists with the first exhibition featuring, no not the first black Jackson *Bollock,* the highly individual, unique never-been-seen-before, Franchot Seaton.'

Tone was now sitting bolt upright, his refilled glass momentarily forgotten. 'Tell me you're kidding me? *Please* tell me you're kidding me? Oh shit! No, you're not kidding! You're fucking serious!'

'Fucking *fucking* serious!' He gave the stunned black man a disarming grin. 'How does Spiers-Seaton Fine Arts sound to you?'

Tone gave a huge, white flashing grin in return. 'Spiers-Seaton F A? I like it, yep! I definitely like it!' before adding, 'But F A, while *you* may see it as standing for Fine Art, it could also stand for *fuck all*!'

'No, I think you really mean *Fucking A*! Trust me, partner-to-be as opposed to bridegroom-to-be. Oh, and whilst we're about it, one fairly important question…'

'And that is?'

'If I'm not hideously mistaken, you are *the* Franchot Seaton, the painter supreme, around whom this whole freaky fetish centres, are you not?'

Tone stuck out his large right hand. 'The best freaky fetish *you'll* ever find! Put it right there, partner!'

'You're going to open an art gallery? That's nice.' The voice came out in a soft whisper.

David Spiers, having taken early retirement (it had been tactfully suggested by his local diocese that he do so) looked adoringly at his blond, tanned nephew. Thanks to Aunt Sybil's life insurance, a small golden handshake plus his pension, the ex-pastor had been able to purchase an adequate two bed-roomed flat within his former parish. The sympathy and generosity of a few of his former loyal parishioners had also helped alleviate the indignity of his sudden dismissal.

'The poor man has never been quite the same since that terrible tragedy involving his wife,' had been Margaret Butterworth's never ending mantra. 'If anyone deserves some Christian charity, *he* most certainly does!'

Aided and abetted by her son, a local estate agent, the kindly woman had not only helped him find the flat but also saw to the decorations. To her chagrin, apart from a polite, brief note thanking her for her help, Margaret Butterworth was never to hear from David Spiers again.

'Better she be surprised by his rudeness than the other!' Jeremy had laughing confided to Tone. 'If bosomy Butterworth ever does decide to pay an impromptu call, the other surprise of finding Aunt Sybil instead of the ex-reverend could be a bit much for the interfering old cunt!'

'How *is* Sybil?'

'Trying, Tone, *very* trying and not in the way of being helpful!' Jeremy couldn't resist a snigger. 'Ever since I got the old queen into wifey's drag, she's been as happy as a sow in shit! She spends all her time getting the most outrageous gear through those mail order catalogues. Jesus, Tone, yesterday she appeared for breakfast in a sequinned *cocktail dress*! I kid you not! Bright red sequins are not compatible with tea, toast and marmalade.'

'Do you still... er, do the business?'

'But of course! Sybil's ever so experimental – not only is it *Gay Tube* and more on the computer, but DVDS galore! She's gone from wallowing under my golden showers to hearty scat sandwiches. It'll no doubt be pee, toast and shit next for breakfast!'

'Jesus, Jer...'

'I know, I know Tone. Quite delectable, aren't I?'

'So, you're going to open a gallery?' The question had been quietly repeated, Sybil then taking a dainty sip of his (for the moment still Earl Grey) tea. 'Where dear?' The second question coming out in a tremulous quaver.

'In London, Sybil. No point in opening anything up here – unless it's your arse!'

'Oh Jeremy!' tittered the elderly man, shaking his bald head, his brass hoop earrings jangling. 'You can be so wicked with your words!'

His uncle's watery eyes suddenly became more watery than usual. 'Oh dear, does that mean...'

'Yes, Sybil. I'm moving to London to get away from this fuck heap of a town and especially all these fuck awful northerners.'

'Oh dear, dear,' came the almost inaudible reply. 'Now that wasn't a very nice thing to say, not a nice thing at all... When you think...'

'Don't *quibble,* Sybil!' snapped his nephew. 'And, as I've told you numerous times before, listen before you speak! I didn't say *you* fuck awful northerners, I said *these* fuck awful northerners.' He looked at David's heavily made up face, the tears now openly carousing down his rouged cheeks. 'What on *earth* makes you think that I'd be leaving you here?'

'You mean?'

'Sybil!' Jeremy gave an exaggerated sigh as if speaking to an errant child. 'The Spiers-Seaton gallery is to be a one off, and to be a one off, you have to have more than those old chestnuts! Unique? Startling? Avant-garde? What do these words mean? Zilch! Nothing! *Nada*! It's all tired old, old crap. No Sybil the quibble, we are going to be *fuck-fantasy-fantastic*!'

He pointed sternly at the now bug-eyed old queen – in his excitement Sybil had allowed his lurex stole to slip, exposing his bony shoulders and sparse grey-haired chest – 'You've wowed them in the aisles! You're people friendly. Why, you've sold the greatest commodity of them all! God and his closet-queen of a son! And that takes some sales speak! What more could my partner and I ask for?' Jeremy, now standing, took a theatrical stance and, pointing his arm at the visibly quivering old man, cried dramatically. 'So, may I, per-lease, ladies and gentlemen, voyeurs, sickos, weirdoes and all, introduce you to Madame Sybil Spiers, gallery *directrice* supreme!'

'Oh my!' gasped Sybil, clutching wildly at the lurex stole which had slid down even further in his shimmying of excitement. 'Oh, my, my, my, my, *my*!'

'Yes, Sybil. Tone – Franchot Seaton – and I have given the ambience, the *look* to the gallery a great deal of thought. We need you as part of the *fuck-fantasy-fantastic*! We need an atrocity – *you* to be exact – in all her giddiest finery but a *giddy aunt* with aplomb! An Auntie Mame of the *mortification*! You will epitomise asceticism. You will walk through fire, endure self flagellation *and even lie on nails* to ensure *F F F* is *F F F!*'

'Oh my!'

'You will meet, greet, horrify, repel, appeal and therefore seduce all our potential purchasers. Your moment of triumph, your ultimate *mental* orgasm will be when you *stick a red dot* on a painting sold!'

'Oh my, my, my…!' croaked Sybil, the forgotten stole now on the floor. 'Oh my!'

'May I take it that your diarrhoeic use of "of my" is an "oh yes?"'

'Oh yes!' croaked Sybil, his claw-like hands now clutching the large golden plastic crucifix at his throat. 'Oh yes!' Giving Jeremy an arch look, the old man couldn't help asking, 'And perhaps a cup of warm wee wee to celebrate?'

'I thought you'd never ask!' smirked Jeremy, unzipping his fly.

It had been Tone's idea for Sybil to be used as a figurehead for the gallery. 'Let's face it, like those carved heads on the prow of old sailing ships, the more ornate, the more over the top, the more prosperous and successful we'll look! Sybil's a figurehead just waiting to sail! She's outrageous enough in mail order schmutter, imagine her with some real money to spend? Any ostrich with any sense of preservation will be heading for the hills! The old thing will relish the role, adores you and will be in her penultimate heaven.'

'Wow! That's quite a speech for a Rasta-who-never-was, Tone boy! Which dictionary did you secretly swallow?'

'It's hanging round you, bwana, and picking up your dropped pearls of shit!'

'Oh, c'mon Tone, we all know you were the secret school swot until Charlie became your darlin'!'

'Charlie never became *my* darlin', darlin'! Charlie just became my sugar daddy!'

'But are you sure, Tone? About Sybil?'

'Trust me Jer, have I ever been wrong when my big black hose – I mean *nose* – begins to twitch? Mark my words, Sybil Quibble will end up being a bigger draw than Franchot Bollock or you!'

CHAPTER 5

LONDON – ONE YEAR LATER:

The invitations were distinctive – a matt black tombstone-shaped card edged with a double banding in bronze and red. Instead of an epitaph was the name, Spiers-Seaton Fine Arts, in alternating bronze and red lettering with the birth and death dates being replaced by words detailing the forthcoming opening of Tone's exhibition.

'Fucking A, man!' said Tone on seeing a proof sample. 'Fucking A! Well done Jer, the shape – well, it's cool, really cool!'

'It simply had to be,' said Jeremy, modestly, 'and let's not forget Sybil's vital input! Because of her it's the bronze goddess look instead of the golden oldie look. As you well know, I wanted gold but, for once, Sybil's quibbles won the day!'

'Dare I say bronze *wonz*?' quipped a grinning Tone.

'Oh Franchot, you are *so* funny!' tittered Sybil. 'How I *adore* that black humour of yours!'

'But look at you too!' cut in Jeremy before Tone could come back with some sharp reply to Sybil's obvious intentional double entendre. 'Aren't you just the business? Isn't Sybil just the business, Tone?'

'Oh *stop*, Jeremy! You know when you say such things I get all hot and bothered under the collar.' He gave a giggle. 'Which is no longer – thanks to you – that wretched dog collar!'

'Not from what I hear,' quipped Tone, determined not to let Sybil get the better of them. 'Rumour has it you get really hot with another sort of collar and requisite lead!'

'Only on a Sunday, Franchot dear,' came the crisp reply. 'That's when Sybil likes her Jeremy to take her walkies!'

'Walkies! Talkies! Enough, you two.' Jeremy shook his blond head in mock exasperation. 'Jesus wept! It's either a case of "Don't quibble, Sybil!" or "cut the moan, Tone!"'

'So, what do you think of your *directrice's* little number for our grand opening?' – here Sybil looked at the large bronze watch, made in the shape of a curled turd by one of their new friends, a fashion designer with the improbable name of Butch Scatt – 'which, if my turd serves me well, is in approximately thirty minutes time.'

'You'll probably be the first one to receive a red dot!' laughed Tone. 'And if, by chance, it's stuck on your forehead, you may then even be mistaken for Bollywood Goes Very Good!"'

'Why, thank you, big, beautiful Franchot. I'll take that a gracious compliment of sorts, if I may. After all, an old maharanee like myself must do all she can to *curry* favour!'

'Now stop it you two!' laughed Jeremy. He looked at his uncle, standing in a camp, mannequin-style pose in front of him and Tone. Who would have ever thought, he said to himself, a smile of pure admiration plus delight on his handsome face. Who would have ever imagined that dreary, timid, David Spiers had been hiding this madcap inner being within himself for all those years? 'Sybil,' he said out loud. 'You would launch ten thousand ships forget the paltry one thousand!'

'Did you say quips?' asked Tone, attempting to keep a straight face.

'Lucky for you, Franchot dear, I'm a lady otherwise I may have taken on the impossible task of trying to give you a black eye!'

'Touché!' Tone gave the little man a mischievous smile. 'We know Mr Scatt is responsible for the dump on wrist but, pray tell, who is responsible for your get-up? Quite extraordinary that er... dress, if this humble artist may say so!'

'Indeed he may say so!' chirruped Sybil. He did a small pirouette is his high heeled (walrus tusks), red satin shoes. 'But your *directrice* is not wearing a dress for this momentous occasion; see it as more of a shroud! Much more appropriate, don't you think?'

Eyeing the bronze and bright red striped silk off the shoulder, full length creation, Tone could not resist a mumbled, 'You'll knock them dead!'

'Very cryptic!' camped Sybil.

'Just the sort of girl one could take home to mother!' laughed Jeremy.

'Most mothers *I* know are fairly house proud!' This from a now openly laughing Tone.

'Oh! You delicious butch bitch!' camped Sybil, waggling a red gloved finger at him. He looked at the curious watch on his thin wrist. 'I think it's time to take up our positions, boys!' Looking up at the two young men smiling down at him he added softly. 'Thank you both, my dears.'

'Sybil?' This from Jeremy.

'Yes dear?' The little man, about to turn and make his way to the front reception, looked back at his nephew.

'You look great and you're doing us proud. As they say in show biz, *Break a Leg*!'

'Not only a leg, dear,' said his uncle. 'Let's make it the whole fucking bank!' With a flutter of red gloved fingers the little man teetered off.

'Who would have believed it?' muttered Tone, with genuine admiration.

'Certainly not his doppelgänger, Sybil the First!' chuckled Jeremy.

The move to London had proved to be more complicated than anticipated. David Spiers, to his surprise, having put his small flat on the market had sold this – including most of the contents – within a week. Encouraged by this being seen by all three as *a good* sign, they then had the further luck of finding – through a contact of Jeremy's from his school days – a comfortable serviced flat to rent in Chelsea's exclusive Redcliffe Square.

'Hugh Grant's a neighbour!' Tone had boasted to Violet.

'Hugh who?' his mother had questioned. 'If he's from the whisky family then you should make friends, otherwise, forget it!'

'A gallery with a difference? Hmm, isn't that what *everyone* wants these days?' Nigel, the old school friend responsible for the Redcliffe Square flat, eyed Jeremy and Tone seated across from him in the comfortable bar of the Wyndham Grand Hotel set within the luxurious Chelsea Harbour residential and marina complex. Taking a long sip from his vodka tonic, his brow furrowing slightly, he asked the inevitable question. 'How much are you planning on spending?'

Jeremy looked at the pale, plump young man sitting opposite him, immaculate in his dark blue Saville Row suit, Turnbull & Asser shirt and tie plus the de rigueur Gucci loafers along with a pair of garish red and black patterned socks. 'Er... '

'We plan to rent at first,' cut in Tone firmly. 'Then, once things take off, we'll think again.' Contrary to Jeremy's unfaltering belief in his talent, Tone still harboured an innate misgiving about the whole venture. Having been brought up to respect the value of money he could not understand Jeremy's willingness to take a substantial mortgage whereas a short rental would spare any future complications. Their differences had led to several loud arguments prior to another meeting with Nigel.

'Renting could be a problem,' began Nigel but, on seeing Tone's handsome face turning into a scowl, quickly added, 'but I may have an idea!'

'Good.' Said Tone, settling back onto the comfortable sofa and giving Nigel an eyeful of his bulging crotch. Yeah, take a good look podgy Nige, he thought, 'cause that's all you're getting, a look. To add to the young estate agent's flickering glances, Tony raised his pelvis slightly, allowing his massive outlined cock and balls (he was wearing no underpants) to press even more tantalisingly against the thin cotton of his chinos.

Taking his mobile out from his breast pocket, Nigel punched in a number. After a few seconds his call was answered, 'Binny? Nigel Fortesque. How's business?' The young man chatted for a few moments before changing tactic and asking, 'Bins, those old undertakers' premises near Lots Road, remember them? Yup, that's right, they were closed after it was discovered the owner was doing much more to his clientele than simply preparing them for their grand finale! That's right, *Nick The Nec,* as one of the tabloids described him!' Nigel turned to a bemused Jeremy and Tone. 'Nic the Nec, short for Nic the necrophiliac, the former owner. Apparently he'd been happily fucking all his clients, male and female, for years before being caught while on the job. A case of *corpus interruptus,* no doubt?' He gave a braying laugh before putting the phone back against his ear.

Occasionally nodding his head he listened for a few minutes more before giving out another loud laugh. 'So, still vacant, Bins? What's that, ah, very funny Bins, very funny!' Pulling a face, he added. '*Still desecrated as opposed to consecrated*? Oh, I'm sure the clients will simply collapse at *that* little bon mot! In fact, I'm sitting with the two guys who may be interested in renting something exactly like this! Yes, they want to rent as opposed to buy. For how long?' Giles raised a questioning eyebrow at Jeremy and Tone as Tone held up his large hand, his five fingers outstretched. 'Five years max. Can you get back to me? Oh sure, if you think it's a goer we can be there in like ten minutes. We just happen to be up at the Wyndham Grand as we speak.'

Three hours later, Dean & Sons, Undertakers, a defunct but spacious, if somewhat rundown building set in a quiet cul-de-sac off the busy Lots Road, Chelsea Harbour, had two new owners.

Binny, who turned out to be a blonde, vivacious tiny dyke dressed in a vibrant mauve trouser suit and matching pixie boots, mesmerised the two young men with her quick-fire, camp sales talk.

'Herewith the fuckery!' she had chortled, showing a small, private room, 'as opposed to the muckery! The fuckery being where the cadavers were given that final, very personal, touch by Nick the Nec before being boxed!'

'Did he really screw *all* the corpses?' This from an intrigued Tone.

'Most of them,' replied Binny, her face deadpan. 'Quite a sad story, if you care to dig deep!' She gave a camp snigger. 'Rumour has it, it all stemmed from the trauma of his wedding night! Apparently, his blushing bride who had been saving herself for the momentous invasion of her sacred hymen, wasn't quite as responsive as our Nick had anticipated. Our hero – or so the story goes – on leaving the still virginal *intactus* Mrs Nec to either ring mummy or else continue to shriek about the invasion of her womb tomb, goes on a monumental piss up and, coming back *here* in a drunken state, then proceeds to mount the obliging corpse of a Mrs Natasha Mowbray, a comely woman conveniently laid out – courtesy of a sudden heart attack – in *acceptus moodus,* and is hooked! Nic would openly brag that he got more *gravefucation* – his word, not mine! – from the likes of Mrs M and her successors, than from his hallowed, if not fallowed, bride!'

'And Mrs Nec?' This from an openly laughing Jeremy.

'Divorced – took the veil.'

'But he fucked the guys as well, didn't he?' This from a wide-eyed Tone.

'Oh, most definitely!' laughed Binny, her blue eyes twinkling. 'To quote Nic the Nec once more, *Too many ladies could become dead boring so I'd switch to drilling the gents. Front or back there was no slack*!'

Having arranged to meet the two back at her offices in nearby Parsons Green to finalise the deal, Binny and Giles had left the two proud owners to survey their new premises. Without hesitation Jeremy and Tone had celebrated with a *Thank you Nic the Nec* fuck in the previous owner's hallowed sanctum.

'And if you say I'm dead boring,' grunted Tone through gritted teeth has he humped and pumped his way into a writhing, groaning Jeremy, 'I'll stick you in one of those refrigerators behind you and, after you're really chilled out, I'll see if old Nic was right, after *all*!' The 'all' came out with a loud gasp as Tone bucked and jettisoned into an equally gasping Jeremy whose hot cum splattered liberally on the tense, black, rippling stomach above him.

'Not dead boring at all!' laughed Jeremy as they quickly cleaned themselves off in a nearby sink. 'Quite the opposite, my friend. More zeppelin man as opposed to zero man!'

'You're not too bad yourself,' laughed Tone. He looked round the small dark room lined with its refrigerated filing cabinets. 'Jesus, Jer, you don't think there's a left over corpse or two in those, do you?'

'For fuck's sake, Tone. That's tomorrows problem but' – and here he shook a playful finger at his grinning friend – 'if there just so happens to be another Mrs M or cool looking gent, no way José!'

'An artist can dream,' laughed Tone.

'Howzit going?'

'Unreal, Tone! Unreal! Apart from two paintings all have been bought. And look at this crowd! London's crème de la crème, the towns hottest A list and all thanks to magical Marky – and you! Who could ever say a good buggering education doesn't pay.' The benefactor of the aforesaid education being another ex-school friend of Jeremy's, a public relations supremo, one Mark Halliday.

'Likewise a good buggering!'

'Touché, Tone. Touché!'

The chemistry between the gigantic, black Tone and the chunky, dynamic Mark at the initial business meeting between the three, had been obvious with Tone responding unashamedly to the young man's blatant eye contact.

'He's asked me out to dinner tomorrow,' Tone whispered as Mark had made his way unsteadily to the Gents, the effects of five double Martinis starting to take their toll. 'If duty calls and I'm expected to wave my big black wand to sweeten the deal he's obviously about to offer, I take it my partner has no objections?'

'Duty first! Self second!' camped Jeremy in a brilliant send up of the present Queen Elizabeth. 'My husband and I, like the rest of our parasitic relations, believe in fucking for freebies! Long may we gain!' He gave his partner a broad wink. 'Wave that big black wand like a fucking propeller, if you have to partner! As long as it gets us what we want!' He nodded in the direction of the bar entrance. 'Careful, the sacrificial scam is on his way back.'

'What I like about my partner,' said Tone, studying his now empty glass. 'Is his liberal thinking regarding my dick.'

'Liberal thinking? Let's face it Tone, that dick of yours has been more liberal than a rabid rabbit on speed! It's up to you, Franchot.'

'What about another round of these?' said Mark now again sitting comfortably. Looking directly at Tone's crotch he couldn't resist a drunken snigger. 'Or should that be one for the load?'

Mark had invited Tony to *The Troubadour,* a popular jazz club restaurant in Kensington and a favourite of Prince Harry. The fact that it was only a few minutes walk from the rented flat in Redcliffe Square had not gone unnoticed by Jeremy and Tone.

'I'll diplomatically be out with Sybil so the flat is yours for putting penis to paper for the final details!' Jeremy had quipped. 'The dizzy old thing's determined to salivate for a fucking third time over Mr Firth being *A Single Man.* I'll then take her onto *Scalini's* for dinner where she can drool over the moustached Vallerio, the macho maitre d'! Christ, the old thing's *insatiable* since she deigned to step out of the Ark! We'll be back by midnight, no later Cinders! So make sure that our dirty deal is well and truly sealed.

'I'll do my best to make sure it's well and truly *semen*-ted!' laughed the big black man.

Tone, not one to believe in making any small talk, had come directly to the point with Mark. 'OK Marky,' he said, the two now on their second bottle of wine and dinner finally ordered, 'What are you offering?'

'More to the point, what are *you* prepared to offer?' smirked the young man, his blue eyes glittering mischievously in the candlelight.

'If your offer sounds worthwhile then I'm prepared to offer ten, thick black inches in return and a fuck to remember!'

'Here's the deal,' said Mark, not missing a beat. Reaching into the inside pocket of his blazer, he produced a sheaf of folded paper and handed these over to Tone. The first page gave a list of names which, to a novice like Tone, held no interest. 'So?' he asked. 'Where are the names?'

'The names on that list, my friend, are the best you could ever hope for. That is money with a capital M and a purchasing power that is second to none. Forget you café society cunts along with the even more nebulous – what I call – Nescafe society. All instant muck, desperate to be seen, be obscene plus eat and drink as much as they can while giving nothing in return. Be warned, London harbours them by the hundreds!'

'Here,' he pointed to another page consisting of only six names. 'This little lot are priceless, six of London's top, most revered art critics. I'll organise a lunch, somewhere expensive and very discreet. Harry may come here but we'll go to where granny sometimes ventures forth, Bellamy's in Mayfair. Here, these six will meet you *before* the gallery opening but only as faces to a name, there will be no sales spiel about what they will be seeing on the night of nights! Woo and they'll pursue, mark my words!'

Mark took another sip of his wine (Tone discreetly beckoning for a further bottle). 'Now, I know you've gotten yourselves an old funeral parlour and, apart from you and your paintings, what else?'

'Sybil!'

'Sybil?'

'Sybil, our mascot.' Our *directrice* extraordinaire!' With genuine delight Tone went on to describe the phenomenon of David Spiers.

'That's it!' cried Mark, waving his excitedly and narrowly missing the third bottle about to be poured, their main course sitting untouched in front of them. 'The second coming; from priest to High Priestess!' He gave a lopsided leer, 'The a-tone-ment sublime!'

'Franchot, Franchot Tone Atonement Seaton,' chuckled Tone.

'Even better,' laughed Mark. He raised his glass. 'Franchot to franchise! Christ goes commercial! God goes for gold! Tone, my friend. Leave it me!'

An hour later a gasping Mark, his hands scrabbling to support his weight on the mattress, was literally lifted off his knees by Tone's fist deeply embedded up his arse. While the young man had screamed hoarsely as Tone pounded him relentlessly with his thick, rigid ten inch length (Mark being on his back, his legs held wide apart between Tone's broad, sweating shoulders), it was obvious that he was looking for even more. Lying panting alongside the equally heavy breathing

Tone, Mark had slyly asked, 'That was great, fucking great but er…
you don't have any toys around, do you? Something bigger?'

'You into fisting?' came the growled response.

'I've only tried it once but, Christ Tone!' he glanced down at
the man's enormous hand lying against his thick, flaccid black cock,
'That's not a fist, it's more of a bloody medieval mace!'

'Hey, not so much of the medieval! C'mon, young Mark…'
Tone leaned across and fumbled in the bedside cabinet drawer. 'It just
so happens that there is something in here to assist the fist! Let you
embrace that mace! On your knees Marky boy! Uncle Tone is going
in slowly and then, my friend, it's hold onto your fucking tonsils!'

'How did it go?'

'A brilliantly done deal, even though I say it myself!' Tone
smiled at Sybil and Jeremy sitting opposite him, a large nightcap of
Courvoisier brandy in their respective hands. 'I also have a feeling
our young Mr Halliday will be sitting side saddle for the next few
days.' The big man gave a laugh. 'When all was done and dusted he
insisted on me going right up to my elbow…'

'Jesus!'

'Jesus, Joseph and even Mary have nothing to do with it!
That guy could handle bloody Eurostar!' Tone laughed again before
smoothing out the several lists on the coffee table. 'Apart from the
movers and shakers, we, my dears – once a date has been established
for our grand opening – are to host a lunch party for a group of art
critics who will either make or break us! The venue – which Mark will
set up – is none other than Bellamy's where the real queen sometimes
drops by for a simple snack! To put it in our nut sacs, we are, dear
comrades in charms, on!'

'Sybil, my dear, a vision! A total vision! Why, if you were
hanging on the wall I'd buy you myself!'

'Oh Giles!' Sybil gave a discreet lady-like titter. 'I bet you say
that to all the girls!'

'Oh Sybil, dear Sybil. But don't forget, I know your secret! I
know you are not like all the other girls but to me, that doesn't matter!
To me you are my Circe, Cleopatra and Clytemnestra all deliciously

packaged into one delicious cornucopia of heavenly delights!' Giles Delaware, art critic *formidable,* bon vivant and a well-known ladies man, stood gazing at Sybil, looking more like a mischievous gnome than the vindictive, spiteful man he supposedly was. White haired, perfectly groomed and carrying his de rigueur silver-topped cane, he was the epitome of elegance.

'Oh Giles!' tittered Sybil again. 'Next you'll be saying you even approve of these paintings *on* the walls! The works by our divine Franchot Seaton. You can be *such* a flatterer!'

'Flatterer! Smatterer! Who cares! But if you want my real opinion on your protégé, that glorious piece of ebony standing over there? Well, I'll tell you, my Sybil divine.' Giles Delaware took a deep breath as Sybil held his. 'In his weekend column, the revered, worshipped and on occasions despised Giles Delaware will announce the arrival of Mr Franchot Tone on the London art scene – however, not merely an arrival but an explosion of meteorites as not being seen here in the past twenty years!'

'Oh my…' whispered Sybil, a red gloved hand to his throat. 'Oh my, my, my, my…!

'I take it that recurring *oh my* is a good sign?' Jeremy, who had been hovering nearby watching Sybil and the formidable art critic deep in conversation, thought it time to intervene. Giving Giles his most charming smile, he continued. 'What have you been saying Mr Delaware? Our Sybil has gone quite pink!'

'Ah, Jeremy!' Giles Delaware gave a warm smile as opposed to his usual thin one (So much for his reputation as Disastrous Delaware, mused Jeremy). 'As I've said to you at that charming luncheon you gave last week, it's Giles, *not* Mr Delaware.' He took a sip from his champagne flute. 'Now we're back on intimate terms… I was just saying to the ravishing Sybil that this is a night to be remembered. Tonight the art world has a new star in its firmament! Your Franchot Seaton – mark my words – will within *months,* not years, have superseded the likes of Mr Francis Bacon and Mr Jackson Pollock, both whom I believe to be the greatest painters of the last century. I must confess I detect the influence of both in Mr Seaton's work but then the man is young and the young develop. I cannot wait to see what Franchot Seaton comes up with in a few years from now.' He touched

Jeremy lightly on the arm with the stem of his champagne flute while gently stroking Sybil's glove with his free hand. 'Remember tonight in the years to come. The first in future nights of many, many similar triumphs!'

True to his word, Giles Delaware, along with the other chosen five, had nothing but praise for the new Franchot Seaton.

Unbeknown to these masters of 'make or break,' and emergency meeting had been held in the gallery the following morning.

'How quickly can you get out another six to eight canvasses, Tone? It took you a year to get this exhibition together so we're talking several months, are we not?'

Tone nodded in the direction of Sybil who was busy mixing a jug of Bloody Marys in the small kitchenette off the office.

'Why not check with Sybil?' he said.

'Sybil? Why, what's she got to do with it?

'You don't, for one moment, seriously think all these paintings on show were all mine, do you?'

'Wha…what do you mean?' stammered Jeremy.

'Jesus Jer, when we decided on this gallery lark you didn't really expect me to give up all my nice little earners and knuckle down to my art did you? Hell no, while you've been busy running around chasing the likes of Mark *fist-fuck-me-hard* Halliday and more, this man has been seeing to his own business. If you want a few more Franchot Seatons run off, you'd better ask the real McCoy over there, the lovely Sybil!'

'You called?' cooed Sybil aka David Spiers aka Franchot Seaton and counterfeit artist supreme.

CHAPTER 6

'Fucking cunt stretchers! Yeah, I'm talking about that fucking yowling brat seated next to you, madam! If you'd had any sense of decency – looking at *your* fucking awful excuse for a face – you would have had the fucking thing aborted!'

Howie Carpenter continued to glare at the woman, sitting gawking, open-mouthed at his tirade. 'And another bit of advice, *madam,* close your mouth like you should have closed your legs!'

'Oh!' gasped the woman. 'Oh!' Looking wildly around the pretentious so-called bar restaurant, she gestured weakly for the manageress, a thin, sour-faced woman standing staring vacantly into space alongside the till. 'Excuse me! Excuse me!' squawked the flustered woman. 'Excuse me!'

'Nothing could excuse you, *cunt*!' snarled Howie rising to his feet and glaring down at the now cowering subject of his scorn. Giving her a slow, deliberate 'fuck you' sign with his two fingers he turned to leave but not before adding. 'And since you seem to think it your right to ruin everyone's day with that disgusting cunt spew of yours, I suggest you pay my fucking bill.' Turning to the manageress who had finally decided to intervene, Howie pointed a thick, sausage-like finger at her and simply whispered, 'Don't,' before walking calmly through the open door and onto the busy street.

Reaching for his mobile, he punched in a number. 'Change of venue,' he said on the call being answered. 'This fuck heap of a place you suggested, *Balkans* or some such shit? No way José! I'm booted and suited so let's meet at a place of *my* choice! Rib Room Bar, Jameirah Carlton Tower in, say. Half an hour? I'll grab a cab and see you there.'

Settling himself comfortably in the back of a cab – the big man had been amused to see the disparate manageress and some fey waiter peering up the street in the direction he had gone – Howie gave a grunt of satisfaction. 'And just what would you and Peter Pansy have done if you *had* approached me?' he muttered, 'Asked to play with my magic wand? Useless, pathetic shits!'

Howie Carpenter – a six foot four giant of a man more Neanderthal in appearance than human – billed himself as a 'fixer,' a man of all trades. 'Like my name – sometimes dangerously taken in vain! – so was your phony Jesus one,' he would proudly boast, 'And look what he claimed he could do! However, anything he could do I can do better! Though' – and here his thick, fleshy lips would take on a sinister grimace – 'Whereas that guy was a *do gooder,* I'm the *do badder*!'

Third in a family of eight siblings, the boy had been brought up in one of London's less fortunate areas, the borough of Camberwell. 'Gollywogs and ragheads!' his father, a drunken layabout would loudly proclaim in between beating up his wife and children with regular abandon. Howie, like his elder brother Dan, had learned to fend for himself from an early age. By the time he was seven Howie was a deft hand at shop lifting, handbag snatching and general pilfering. His size belied his age and at the age for seven he was already passing for a thuggish ten to twelve year old.

A visit to the local cinema (he and Dan were experts at sneaking in through a convenient fire door) and seeing Roger Moore as secret agent James Bond, young Howie had decided, there and then, to turn himself into Mr Sinister Suave as opposed to Mr Sinister Schmuck.

Immaculately groomed and a walking advert for any top designer label, Howie made sure he never went unnoticed. The contrast as to when he was fixer as opposed to man-about-town could not have been greater. 'Designer to down market,' he would growl approvingly when viewing the mirrored reflection of a man wearing an old peak cap, battered leather jacket, well-worn jeans and scuffed work boots.

'Mr Carpenter?' The elegant young brunette, immaculate in a cream linen trouser suit and carrying a Prada shoulder bag, stood looking down at the big man glowering at the evening paper.

'You're forty fucking minutes late,' growled Howie, before the unexpected softly spoken voice registered, making him look up with a startled glance. 'I beg your pardon, ma'am,' he said, pulling his heavy frame to his feet, 'I must admit I was expecting someone else!' Holding out a massive, well-manicured hand, he gave his version of what he considered a debonair smile. 'Yes, I am Mr Carpenter and I was expecting a Mr Ted Cooper. If I may say so, you don't *look* like a Ted Cooper, nor do you sound like one!'

'How very reassuring,' came the cool reply. 'May I join you?'

'Please!' Howie gestured to a vacant chair opposite his. 'I haven't ordered a drink as yet as I prefer not to drink alone. I expect your preference will be more er... shall we say, *distinctive,* than the mysterious Mr "call me Ted, mate!" Cooper, so may I take the liberty of ordering us a bottle of champagne?'

'You may indeed, Mr Carpenter.'

'Howie, please!'

'Mary Magdalene,' said the brunette, her pale face deadpan. She reached out with her small hand, lightly touching Howie's, as if giving it her blessing. Sitting herself down elegantly on the bergere-style chair she removed her shoulder bag, placing this on the low table between them. 'And before we even begin to discuss business; a sweetener to show you just how serious we are!' The young woman took out a vellum envelope from within her bag. 'No! Please simply accept it without any further question. If you *do* decide to help us there's obviously more, a great deal more to follow. However, if you simply decide to walk out without hearing what we have in mind, the contents of the envelope should more than compensate for your already wasted time.'

Without uttering a word of thanks Howie simply scooped up the envelope and pocketed it inside his bespoke jacket. Not breaking eye contact with the stunningly attractive woman he muttered his order to a hovering waiter before abruptly saying, 'How did you find me?'

'This may come as a surprise, *Howie,* but it was through the mysterious Ted Cooper. Does the name Thornhill ring any bells?'

'Thornhill? Stephanie Thornhill? The lady living in Monaco? Ah yes, it does ring a bell, a very loud and very definite bell, *Mary*!'

'Good! Stephanie *Fellowes*-Thornhill is the mother of a friend and *she* told me how nasty step-daddy mysteriously disappeared whilst out sailing one day. Daddy's body was never found but mummy Thornhill and daughter have never looked back, if you catch my drift?'

Howie continued staring at the composed young woman. 'Who *are* you?' he demanded.

'I told you, Mary Magdalene, and I'm expecting you to be my saviour!'

Several hours later Jeremy was still trying to come to grips with bombshell that it was Sybil and not Tone responsible for most of the paintings shown in the exhibition.

'But how? When?' he had kept saying over and over again.

'Oh. Don't be such a *cur,* Jer!' camped Sybil, giving a squeak of delight at his wit. 'Whilst Jeremy was out and about, we were both in the rear works studio when Franchot suggested Uncle Sybil try *her* dainty hand at his splish, splash and splatter technique! What really happened was he suggested I do a sort of *painting by numbers,* for every daub, dab or splatter of his, I did the same. It was such *fun*! We'd started on one canvas when Franchot had to go out to meet one of his shady – oh, forgive me Franchot! – friends, so I simply went on and finished it. *In record time*!'

'But which ones are which?' demanded Jeremy, his frustration growing.

'Well, dear,' said Sybil with his sweetest smile, 'If *you* can't tell which is which, then we're certainly not going to!' He looked at a grinning Tone and then back at a seething Jeremy. 'So dear, *don't quibble* with Franchot and Sybil; simply tell us how many Franchot Seatons you require!'

'Shit! Shit! Shit!' shouted Jeremy in exasperation.

'Shit? Shit? Shit?' snapped Sybil. 'How dare you, you ungrateful little twerp! Now, pull yourself together Jeremy and stop acting like a spoilt little queen!'

Jeremy looked at his tiny, Pucci garbed uncle as if he'd been slapped. '*What* did you say?' he managed to gasp.

'I told you to pull yourself together and to behave! Now, Franchot and I have work to do so why don't you take yourself along the office, sit yourself down in front of the computer and have a nice orgasm whilst working out all that lovely lolly your sweet Uncle Sybil and Franchot are about to make us!'

Jeremy, a look of total disbelief on his face, remained seated, gazing up at the little man frowning across at him from beneath today's bright red pageboy bob. 'What's happening to you, Uncle David?' he whispered.

'Everything!' said the little old man, leaning across and giving Jeremy a light pinch on the cheek. 'Now, run along like a good diddums and go play *Four and Twenty Blackbirds* or, better still, *The Queen was in her counting house, counting out her money*!'

Tone's photograph, along with those of Jeremy and Sybil, had been prominently featured in several Sunday magazines and various tabloids. Tone, with his dashing good looks – 'Think Denzil Washington meets Barack Obama!' as one caption put it! – flashing smile and natural charisma soon found himself the *Painter Pop Star* to teenagers along with a fawning following of men and women across the country.

Young girls would drop by the gallery on the pretext of viewing the exhibition and their disappointment at not seeing the *Fab Franchot Seaton* in person would be obvious. On the few occasions Tone did appear in paint spattered jeans and an artistically torn T shirt, the gallery would be filled with high pitched screams of delight. Sybil was viewed more as a curiosity or, as one pimply miss put it, 'a dotty old lady!' Fan mail for both Sybil and Tone began arriving by the sack load, much to the amusement of the two and much to Jeremy's growing resentment.

'You're becoming more like fucking *Tweedle Dum and Tweedle Dee* every fucking day!' he began to grumble.

'Oh, hark at *Alice, all spite and malice*!' had been Sybil's sharp put down.

Again, several television channels had filmed and interviewed Tone while at work in his studio and it was not long before the banter between the artist and his bizarre *directrice* began to seduce a bemused cult following. 'Franchot's Lucky Shot' with a picture of Sybil perched on an easel alongside the artist had seen Jeremy apoplectic with rage. 'You're meant to be an artist, not a fucking vaudeville act!' he'd screamed.

'Did you hear something, Franchot dear?' had been Sybil's light hearted response, a small hand held to his pendant earring.

To quote Sybil in one of his more pensive moments, the little old man had shyly confided to the devoted Tone, 'I have, dear, at long last found my true heaven here on earth, thanks to my two angels!' Tone meanwhile, seemed unstoppable with his *pop star painter* status ever growing.

Jeremy, now in a serious quandary about what appeared to be his diminishing status within Spiers-Seaton, decided to speak openly to Mark Halliday about the escalating situation. Mark had proven to be a sympathetic listener. Having initially seduced Tone, the young man had firmly believed that from a one night stand something more fulfilling would have developed. As he had once told Jeremy in a depressed, drunken phone call, 'I'm in love with the guy; I'm besotted with the bastard and it's driving me insane!'

Tone had cruelly rebuffed any further advances by ignoring phone messages and being offhand to the extent of blatantly rude to Mark when the two did bump into each other, the exhibition being a prime example where Tone had deliberately snubbed the smitten young man. To find a soul mate in Jeremy was the answer to Mark's prayers.

'He's getting far too big – no, make that, he already gotten – too big for his fucking boots!' sniffed Jeremy, taking a large gulp of his vodka tonic.

'Don't they all?' snorted Mark. 'Give them a taste of the good life or a taste of power… I mean, is there anything more offensive to you, more vomit making than a black traffic warden? Sodding jungle bunnies, they all think they're beyond reproach.' Mark gave another snort. 'I mean, it's reached the stage in this godforsaken country that they're treated like a protected species!'

At Jeremy's suggestion, the two had met up at the bar of his favourite Wyndham Grand Hotel overlooking the marina at Chelsea Harbour. 'Isn't there a chance that Tone may drop by?' Mark had questioned.

'Oh no, it's too local for Mr Franchot bloody Seaton! Nowadays it's nothing less than The Ivy, The Wolseley or the bar at Claridges for our boy!' had been the snapped reply.

'Uppity sod!' spat out Mark.

'And that's putting it politely,' muttered Jeremy. He took another slow, thoughtful sip. 'How trustworthy are you, Marky?' he suddenly asked.

'Trustworthy? Why?' Mark was too taken aback to offer any resentment at such a personal question.

'Because I'm about to ask you to assist me in something that require complete and utter discretion. And something that could be incredibly beneficial to the two of us.' He gave the intrigued young man one of his terrifying laser-like stares. 'By beneficial I mean money, filthy lucre and lots of it!'

'Tell me more,' said Mark, adding, 'And if you're thinking what I'm thinking, I'm your man!'

Still staring at the young man with a blue-eyed intensity, Jeremy slowly leaned forwards and for the next five minutes spoke softly and succinctly to a growingly excited Mark. 'So what do you say?' he ended, leaning back once more into his chair.

'Say? I think you're a fucking lunatic! A total, devious, vile insidious shit! But, if you *are* serious, count me in!' Mark held out his chunky hand which was grasped firmly in return.

Looking down at the two gripped hands, Jeremy returned his gaze to Mark, a small smile playing on his sculpted lips. Once again he glanced back down at their two, still entwined hands before looking back up at Mark who was eyeing him curiously. 'I hear you have a penchant for the odd fist now and then?' he whispered.

Mark, turning a deep crimson, swallowed awkwardly. 'I suppose that bastard went and told you?'

'But of course! Discretion is not part of Mr Seaton's valour.' Giving another smile, Jeremy finally released Mark's hand before making a fist with his own. 'If you're willing...' he began.

'Where and when?' stammered Mark, now acutely embarrassed.

'Why not the gallery? Nobody's there at the moment and Nic the Nec's fuckery is still as he left it. It's the one room we didn't change.'

'Let me get the bill!'

'Oh, and Marky...'

'Yes?'

'A thought! Two hands together?'

'An answer to my fisting prayers!' croaked Mark getting to his feet, his furious erection blatantly apparent. 'Let's get the hell out of here!' he stuttered, throwing a fifty pound note on the table.

'Howie? Mary. Sorry I can't personally oblige but, let the ravishing begin!'

A smiling Jeremy observed the three faces staring at him across his desk. 'Thanks for making time to see me and Marky at such short notice Tone and Franchot Seaton the second!' He gave the bored-looking Tone and serious Sybil a mischievous wink. 'You *do* remember Mark, Tone and Sybil? He's the genius who found us this little gold mine where we're sitting so comfortably today.'

'Can you get to the point, Jer,' mumbled Tone. 'Sybil and I have work to do!'

'Oh?' Jeremy feigned surprise. 'Sybil *and* you? I'm pleased to hear it!'

'Do get on with what you're obviously dying to say,' said Sybil nervously as he eyed the tensing Tone.

'I know you've *both* been busy getting a new set of paintings together,' said Jeremy ignoring Tone's growing anger at his dripping sarcasm. 'And this is a key factor as to why we're here this morning along with Mark.' He reached over to a pile of open letters alongside him and, waving it lightly above his head simply said, 'One of many.'

'What, more fan mail?' sniped Tone, crossing his massive thighs more out of maliciousness to taunt Mark as opposed to making himself more comfortable.

'No, galleries! Galleries galore! Galleries in Paris, New York, Palm Beach, Chicago – you name it – all wanting to purchase a Franchot Seaton or, better still, have the privilege of holding a Franchot Seaton exhibition.' He tapped the pile with a long finger. 'So, what do we do? Just what-do-we-do?'

'So what *do we* do?' chorused Tone, stifling a yawn.

'Paint, Tone Paint! That's what you and Sybil are going to do! No more partying, no more shilly – shallying, the two of you are going to be painting from dawn till dusk until I say stop! Uh! Uh!' he held up a placating hand as a furious Tone started to get up from his seat. 'Do this for me, for us! Jer, Tone and Sybil! *Then* the partying can begin. Mark is here to help us build up the biggest nest egg since Damien Hirst!' Seeing he had at last gained Tone's attention, Jeremy continued. 'In the past few days you've produced six paintings. Spiers-Seaton wants *one hundred and six* and maybe more!'

'Impossible!' snapped Tone. 'As it so happens I don't have the time and to be quite honest, nor the inclination!'

Seeing Jeremy's expression Sybil briskly cut in. 'Ah, but I do! And furthermore, I've got that nice young man helping me!'

'What nice young man?' cried Jeremy in alarm.

'Why, the one who came to the gallery a few weeks ago looking for a job, any sort of job as long as it was in a gallery. Tone saw him with me and gave him one!'

'Gave him one?'

'A job, Jer. Not a bloody fuck!'

'Shut up Tone!' Jeremy glared at the sulky black man and a defiant Sybil. 'You mean you've gone and employed a fourth person here, apart from Alexis our receptionist, at *our* gallery, without my knowledge?'

'Yes, rather like you taking on Mark to do PR without mine and Tone's knowledge!' snapped Sybil.

Tone remained silent, glaring malevolently at his partner.

'Well, have you nothing to say?' spat out Jeremy, glaring at Tone and ignoring Sybil's remark. 'Cat got that over active tongue?'

'Listen to him,' said Tone to no one in particular. 'In one breath he tells me to shut up and when I do, he insults me!'

'Oh, don't go all fucking black on me!' yelled Jeremy. Struggling to regain his composure and ignoring a now silently giggling Tone and Sybil he said slowly and determinedly through gritted teeth. '*Who-is-this-young-man*?'

'Me, Mr Spiers,' said a soft, melodious voice.

Jeremy spun round in the direction of the voice. Standing alongside the open door – Jeremy, in the midst of his tirade against Tone and Sybil had not seen him quietly entering the office – was a slim, dark-haired young man.

'I'm sorry I'm late,' the young man added apologetically, 'but I was just putting some finishing touches to a painting.' He gave a tremulous smile. 'It's such an honour to meet you at last!' Giving a light, almost girlish giggle, the young man added, 'I really *have* been trying to introduce myself but Sybil's such a slave driver! She never allows me a minute away from my work!'

'How long has he been working here?' thundered Jeremy, turning his wrath back onto the now openly giggling two while a tight-lipped Mark sat watching. His fact white with rage, Jeremy then shouted with as much venom as he could muster. 'You do realise this could scupper all our plans?'

'Scupper? Now there's a voice from the past,' guffawed Tone, ignoring the furious face in front of him.

'Shut the fuck up! Tone!'

'There he goes again,' laughed Tone, giving a dismissive shrug. 'OK! OK! Take it that these lascivious lips will remain well and truly sealed!'

'Cunt,' muttered Jeremy. Turning again to the by now thoroughly bewildered young man. 'And as for you, Mr "Any fucking any job will do!" Who are you and why are you really here?'

'Stop it, Jeremy! Stop it *at once*!' A thoroughly furious Sybil had suddenly leapt to his feet and stood glaring at his shaking nephew. 'The young man's name is Francis Denning; he's a friend of mine and Farnchot's plus he's a genius. So, nephew dearest, just shut yer fucking cake hole! Geddit?'

Jeremy's immediate reaction was to collapse back into his chair.

'And before you do anything else!' Sybil squeaked, 'you apologise to Francis for your appalling rudeness!'

'I don't apologise…' mumbled Jeremy.

'Then I don't paint another Franchot Seaton for you – ever!' Sybil, his hands on his bony hips, stood glaring defiantly at his scowling nephew.

'I apologise, Francis,' said Jeremy almost inaudibly.

'Good,' said Sybil. 'It wouldn't win you an Oscar but it'll have to do!' He turned to the petrified young man. 'Now Francis, pull up that spare chair and join us. This little get-together sees you involving yourself in more ways than you could ever have imagined!'

Francis Denning, a nineteen year old college graduate with a diploma in Twentieth Century Modernism, had simply appeared at the gallery, along with his portfolio, looking for a job, 'any sort of job!' albeit cleaner, tea boy or general gofer. On Sybil's insistence he had reluctantly opened his portfolio and nervously presented a series of gouaches and two small oil paintings.

'Where did you originally see these, before you copied them?' Sybil demanded, his breath catching in his chest.

'What do you mean, Miss?' the perplexed young man stammered.

'They must be copies of Franchot's works I haven't seen,' Sybil muttered. 'So where did you find the originals?' he demanded again.

'But they're *not* copies, they're mine, all mine! I swear!' the young man insisted, his nervousness turning to indignation.

'But they're pure Franchot Seaton,' said Sybil quietly, 'Uncannily so…'

'And that's why I'm here,' the young Francis said. 'I want to be another Franchot Seaton!'

'So now you know,' said Sybil, 'and as you now want a hundred and six plus Franchot Seatons, Francis and I will produce these for you.' He then flashed the stunned Jeremy a look of pure mischief. 'And it you want one hundred *and fifty* Franchot Seatons all you have to do is ask. Politely!'

CHAPTER 7

'Good morning, Marky! Coffee?'

Morning, Jer.' Mark gave a yawn. 'Up long? I didn't hear you getting up and, more to the point, I didn't *feel* you getting up!'

'Now, now, Marky! Don't be greedy! Even the jerking Jeremy has to have a break!' He smiled at the tousled-headed young man opposite. 'It's worked out ideally, hasn't it? Tone deciding to move out into that vast, old converted warehouse in Battersea. I must say I still find it hard to believe that he invited both Sybil and that dreadful young boy to take up residence with him!'

'By "the boy" I assume you mean young Francis of A-*sissy*?'

'Ha! Brilliant Marky! Fucking little brown-nosing twerp. Note the term *brown* nosing! Probably got his little nose right up Tone's big black "I'm ripe and ready for a rimming" arse in addition to a daily dabbling with the old black magic!' He laughed drily. 'Christ, it wouldn't even surprise me if he wasn't fucking Sybil in between spewing out the Franchot Seatons! Now there's a thought!'

'I doubt it,' laughed Mark. He gave Jeremy a sly look. 'What would you say if I told you I think Sybil is fucking Francis?'

'Don't be disgusting, Marky! Why, that's rather like the proper queeny doing it with one of her corgis!'

'Now that *is* disgusting!' adding *'My corgi and I'* in a camp, refined falsetto. The two laughed happily, relaxed in each other's company, Mark helping himself to another croissant. Contentedly chewing on the tasty pastry, he swallowed the mouthful before saying, 'How many at the last count?'

'Would you believe it, the tiresome threesome are now at number forty two – or were at the last tally – and still "painting strong!"'

'Hmm.' Mark topped up their coffee cups. 'Right, well the Preston Palin Gallery in Sydney are ecstatic at Tone being able to supply them with two works; as are the Sanko Gallery in Shanghai. We've got a gallery in Abu Dhabi desperate for an exhibition so I've guaranteed them *twelve* Franchot Seatons plus the master himself for the opening. Never mind his fee, the anticipated profit from the sales alone is fairly mind blowing!'

'And what about Palm Beach?'

'Take it as done. A deal similar to Abu Dhabi.'

'It really is a case of painting by numbers, isn't it?'

'Just lie back and think of the numbers to our own numbered account in Switzerland instead!'

Tone's cavalier attitude to the finances involving the gallery – a complete turnabout to his former anxieties – had seen Jeremy in complete control of the every growing cash mountain. As long as Tone was able to draw a generous allowance, have the new flat paid for and indulge in the occasional perk – a BMW coupé being one of these – he was, as Jeremy so succinctly put it 'happy as a pig in shit!' Tone's complete lack of awareness of the money being siphoned out of the company account was regarded by Jeremy and Mark with amusement. 'We're getting richer by the minute,' Jeremy would continually mumble into Mark's neck as they lay entwined in bed late at night.

To Jeremy's surprise, after their initial bout of fisting and fucking the two young men had begun spending more time together, not only within the gallery but socially. Mark's glamorous world of public relations saw them attending endless glittering parties, first nights and other such events. 'It's all good for business,' Mark would laughingly admonish when Jeremy moaned about 'another fucking party!'

Mark's prophecy was beginning to pay off. At one cocktail party he had been introduced to glamorous Palm Beach socialite Ivana Trump, ex-wife of the property billionaire Donald Trump, who promised to attend the opening of the Franchot Seaton exhibition at West Palm Beach's prestigious Piper-Hayden Gallery at the end of the year.

Tone moved in his own world along with a hankering for his former, shady past, straying back to his twilight world of dealers and a dubious group in general.

Sybil remained an enigma working happily away on painting after painting along with the doting Francis always by his side – the rapport between the two being almost uncanny. 'They even *know* what the other's thinking,' Tone had confided to Jeremy on one of the rare occasions they now spoke to each other. While Tone was rarely to be seen at the palatial converted warehouse – he had begun spending more time with a mystery friend who lived in London's answer to New York, the sky-scraper dominated Canary Wharf in the redeveloped East End – his strong affection for Sybil and Francis was more that of nephew and favourite aunt with Francis being happily accepted, as a laughing Tone put it, 'Sybil's platonic *very* toy boy!'

'So we're looking at about another year?'

'At least Marky. Maybe more, but I wouldn't push it.'

Mark thought for a moment, 'Therefore I suggest a slight cooling off period, starting as from now. I'll start dropping hints that an exhausted Franchot Seaton is having a quiet rest period before starting work on his exhibition to end *all* exhibitions; a happening to take place before the end of the year. Franchot Seaton's *Modern Master 555 Marathon.*'

'*Modern Master Marathon*? Explain that, my gallant genius!'

'Franchot Seaton will personally open five exhibitions worldwide in *five* days! And I mean worldwide, beginning with London, then Paris, followed by New York, Sydney and Abu Dhabi. Palm Beach will have to wait.'

'Will he be able to do it?'

'I'm sure he'll be able to *do* it but *will* he do it is the big, big question. It'll mean virtually living in aeroplanes with a stop over in each of the cities after London, Paris being the exception as the openings in London and Paris will take place on the same day with New York the following evening!

'And then it's on to Sydney followed by Abu Dhabi?'

'You've got it, Five, Five, Five.'

'Thank Christ you didn't suggest six, six, six!'

'Very funny, or is that an omen?'

'I get the five days and five cities but I don't get the other five?'

'Tone, you, me, Sybil and young Francis.'

'Why the snippy sissy?'

'Because, my dear, I don't trust the little shit with the hold he has over us. I don't want him out of our sight.'

'You don't think…?'

'Yes, I *do* think and Marky I'm never wrong. There's an old saying, *look in your own backyard before you look abroad*! And it's not only young Francis I have my doubts about.'

'Tone wouldn't do anything untoward to spill his very golden apple cart!'

'Don't be so daft, Marky! It's not Tone I'm worried about, it's *Sybil*!'

'*Sybil*?'

'Yes, Mark; dear dotty Sybil. Take it from me that madcap, camp eccentric act is as phony as David Beckham's bulge! I've been seeing a change that's more than a change, it's a fucking freak out! Talk about the *Seven Ages Of Man*! Age one was that of a nervous neurotic priest; age two, a pliant old pouf; age three, a bizarre butterfly emerging from its chrysalis; age four, butterfly becomes a tough, beady old boots; age five, counterfeit artist extraordinaire; age six, hooks up with a toy boy and for age seven, evil! To explain I quote those wise words from the second witch in *Macbeth* – *By the pricking of my thumbs something wicked this way comes.* She and that Francis are up to some serious shit!'

'Jesus!'

'Not Jesus, Marky. Shit!'

'So when are you planning the er... cull?'

'Immediately on our return. Little lost lamb, saintly Francis will quietly disappear and as for poor, dotty, Sybil, we'll have to find something very glamorous to send her on her way.'

'And Tone?'

'The easiest of the three. Successful artist, unable to cope with the pressures of his fame etcetera, etcetera. Poor sod, he does what many of that ridiculous ilk do, he ODs! End of Franchot bloody Seaton.' Jeremy gave a harsh laugh, 'And here the fun starts! To quote dear Sybil, "Oh my, no more Franchot Seatons, *ever*? My oh my, oh my! Doesn't this mean, Jeremy *dear,* that overnight Franchot's paintings will have become virtually priceless?"'

'I love you, Jeremy Spiers!'

'I'm quite fond of you too, Halliday!' Jeremy glanced down at his watch. 'We've got time. Fancy a bit of fisting and a fuck, comrade?'

CHAPTER 8

'We'll simply have to get you a bigger one,' said Sybil, pursing his lips. He looked at the tousled Francis smiling sleepily alongside him. 'C'mon lazy bones! I know it's a Saturday and we're having a much needed day off, but that doesn't mean lying here all morning. Chop, chop, Francis sweetie, get your glorious, pert, delicious bum out of here and fetch your aged, insatiable, disgusting, perverted Svengali a cup of coffee!'

'What big *teeth* you have, grandma!' chortled Francis, throwing aside the duvet and leaping agilely from the large, comfortable bed.

'All the better for gobbling you with, *Little Red Riding Good*!' chuckled Sybil, lying back against the pillows. 'Now, go and get that coffee like a good little sodomite and, if you're very good and don't quibble with Sybil, we will have a day of fun and we *will* buy you a bigger one!'

Picking up the large latex, flex-coloured dildo alongside his scrawny frame, Sybil pointed it in the direction of the door. 'Now shoo!'

A few minutes later Francis was back in bed, two steaming cups of coffee sitting on a tray atop one of the bedside cabinets. Leaning over the young man gave Sybil a tender kiss on his weathered cheek. 'I love you, Sybil,' he whispered, 'I really do.'

'Nonsense!' laughed the delighted old man. 'What you really love is not *moi* but what I exude... glamour, wit, charm and more charm plus the fact I'm a demon with a dildo!'

'Yes,' said Francis teasingly. 'Of course it really because of all that, especially the dildo bit, but you must also understand that, being a sensitive, artistic soul I couldn't think otherwise. Imagine if I'd gone and said I actually preferred sleeping with a raddled old crone?'

'I know it's only small but never-the-less (Sybil couldn't resist a further giggle) for that nasty, nasty remark you're about to rammed up your bum till queeny cum! C'mon! On your hands and knees, Francis! Bum in the air! This old demon with the dildo is going to give you a dil-doddle and a half! Raddled old crone indeed!'

'*Hideous* raddled old crone!' shrieked Francis with anticipated delight and doing as instructed.

Three hours later Sybil and Francis were in the stylish, Art Deco-inspired Rivoli Bar of the Ritz Hotel, two sparkling champagne cocktails on the small lacquered table between them. Sitting on the plush carpet alongside were two bags from Prowler Stores, a leading chain store devoted to gay toys, books, magazines, DVDS and video films.

'It's an *enormous* dildo, Sybil!' said Francis for the umpteenth time, nodding in the direction of one of the packages.

'Don't quibble with Sybil!' trilled the old man, 'and don't knock it until you try it!'

Sybil, dressed in a purple, orange and pink patterned Missoni trouser suit, purple pixie boots and flaunting a bright pink wig had caused a minor sensation as he minced his way through the gilded reception area of the grand hotel, arm in arm with his beautiful, elegant, young male companion.

'It must be that Jason Perry!' one visitor in the lobby was heard to whisper.

'Nonsense dear, it's that Quentin Crisp!'

'Quentin Crisp is *dead,* dear!'

'So is that one by the looks of *it!*'

Turning in their direction a sweetly smiling Sybil carolled loudly. 'Ladies, ladies. Why don't you try, for once, shutting those dried up old cunt holes you apparently both mistake for mouths? Your over-painted labia posing as *lips* merely grate!'

'Oh Sybil!' gasped Francis in between giggles. 'I've said it before and I'll say it again. I love you! Love you! Love you!'

'Bet you say that to all the dildos,' came the cryptic reply. 'Now, how about those champagne cocktails?'

Their second round of cocktails finished and a reassuring third ordered, Sybil took a deep breath before saying, 'Now, being serious my precious Ganymede, my Narcissus, my muse... have you had time to seriously consider what we discussed last night?'

'I have and I think it's brilliant!'

'Good, so now we can go along with plan one. On Wednesday you are to arrange for your friend Bob, the fucker trucker, to collect the pre-rolled and wrapped four rugs along with some other bits and pieces marked for the apartment in Paris. In Paris he'll meet Jeanette, the concierge, who will be expecting him. Bob is to call her when he nears the Rue Michel-Ange in the sixteenth *arrondissement* – that's district for the uninitiated! – Jeanette will let him in and show him where to store the goods until we arrive.

'I've told Jeremy and Mark – can you believe it? Those two are like a pair of ever copulating Siamese twins – attached to each other almost *everywhere* and always at it!' Sybil gave a small giggle. 'Well, the do say forearmed is fore charmed! Oops, did I really say that?' He took a dainty sip of his cocktail. 'As I've said, I've already told the gruesome twosome that we both desperately need a weekend break and where better than the city of ooh la la! Gay *Paree*! We go there weekend after next.'

'And then?'

'And then on to plan two, Francis precious, followed by our grand finale, the unbelievable, totally unacceptable plan three. Oh, just in time!' Sybil smiled up at the handsome waiter. 'Round three? Oh, thank young man and, we'll soon be ready for round four! Planning murder, mayhem and possibly more is thirsty work! So, another two cocktails after these, thank you dear! Goodness, you are indeed a very pretty young man!'

'Of course er... madam,' stammered the waiter, blushing furiously.

A few weeks earlier Sybil, firmly in his role as David, had travelled to Paris for a meeting with a former priest, a Father Gregory who now helped run a hostel for down and outs situated near the elegant 16th district of the city. Father Gregory remained the only contact from David's days within the church. His feeling for the priest was one of sympathy for it was in David that Father Gregory had confessed his sinful desire for young dark skinned boys, 'particularly those from the northern coasts of Africa!' Whether the priest had or was currently fulfilling his desires in the more louche and malodorous sectors of the multi-cultural city, David simply didn't particularly wish to know. However, Father Gregory, always grateful for David's 'sympathetic ear' and therefore willing to assist the former priest in 'any ploy, whatever,' happily agreed to look for a small apartment in and around his district.

A neat, three room rental on the Rue Michel Ange had proved to be the perfect answer. Jeanette, the elderly concierge had been enchanted by the quietly-spoken, dapper little Englishman and his valiant attempts at speaking to her in her own language. 'It's actually for my sister-in-law and her son, my nephew,' he had explained. 'Madam Sybil and Monsieur Francis will be visiting in a few months time!' Meanwhile, he had gone on to say it would be so kind if the charming Madam Jeanette would see several items of furniture safely stored in the bijou apartment until their arrival.

The woman's response had been a simple, 'But of course, Monsieur Spiers!'

A discreet envelope containing a substantial sum of Euros had sealed the deal. Madam Jeanette's reassurances of 'It will be an honour and a pleasure to be looking after Madam Sybil and Monsieur Francois!' saw David barely able to keep a straight face.

'I'm really looking forward to seeing Paris,' announced Francis finishing off his third cocktail.

'As long as you don't become too ambitious and expect to use the Eiffel Tower as a dildo, you'll love it,' sniggered his mother-to-be.

'Howie? Bring me up to date please!'

'And a very good morning to you too, Mary! The latest? Franchot it appears, has been sentenced to six months hard labour!'

'What do you mean?' Mary's voice took on a strident note.

'I mean there's rumour of a major new exhibition in a few months' time involving the whole circus and our Franchot has his big noise to the grindstone or, perhaps that should be easel! Spiers-Seaton Fine Arts are doing a Phileas Fogg-inspired journey only in their case its *Around the World in Five Days* as opposed to eighty!'

'Very droll, Howie! I'm most impressed.'

'Oh, I know my *films*, Mary,' said the big man snidely, thinking, Next the stuck up bitch will be claiming she's bloody Liz Taylor to my Mike Todd! Mary fucking Magdalene, my arse!

'Will this help?'

'It makes it simpler, Mary M, much, much more simpler. Meanwhile I've been looking into their set-up and apart from Spiers and Seaton, obviously, there's a third director, a David Spiers, Jeremy's uncle.' Howie gave a hollow laugh. 'Seems this David Spiers is a bit of an oddball. Wears drag the whole time but has an amazing sales spiel and is seen as an integral part of the business.'

'Ignore David Spiers, he's nothing to do with this! So, when you say this around the world caper makes things simpler, what exactly do you mean?'

'Now Mary M, that would be telling!' Howie gave a small, low rumble of a laugh. 'Rest assured, just leave it up to me and before the end of their trip both you wishes will have been granted.' He gave another laugh, 'Most people settle for three wishes; are you sure you'll be happy with only two?'

'Two fulfilled wishes are more than enough, but thank you for your concern, Howie!'

'And Mary…'

'Take it as done, Howie. The transfer for your next stage payment will be made today, and Howie…'

'Yes, Mary?'

'Please remember that sweetener of ten thousand pounds handed over at our first meeting remains a sweetener and will not be offset against further transactions.'

'Thank you Mary.' There was a moment's pause before Howie continued. 'Do Mary Magdalenes ever eat?'

'I thought you'd never ask!' came the laughing reply.

'This evening?'

'My, you *are* a fast worker! Yes, why not this evening?'

'*Cipriani,* at nine?'

'Lovely.'

Howie couldn't resist another deep laugh. 'I'd offer to collect you but you've never given me your address.'

'Some things Howie are better left unsaid!'

Five hours later, back in his small Mayfair mews house, an exhausted, sweat-drenched Howie, his vast hairy chest still heaving, lay sprawled out against the pale, slim young woman. 'Christ,' he managed to gasp, 'whoever taught you how to fuck deserves a bloody knighthood!'

'Thank you, Howie!' came the laughing reply.

'Who *are* you?' said the big man. 'Just who the fuck *are* you?'

'I've already told you; Mary Magdalene.'

'Then God doesn't know what he's missed! But Christ, what a *mental* fuck!'

Howie had arrived early at the stylish Mayfair eatery and, sitting at the long bar, ordered himself a vodka martini. No doubt she'll be late, like the first time, he was thinking when the now familiar voice said softly, 'Penny for them but I bet they were along the lines, *bet the bitch will be late!*'

'Mary!' Howie, to his immediate surprise found his delight in seeing her again to be spontaneous.

'My, but don't you look…well, you look terrific! Please, take a seat!'

'Why, thank you kind sir! And so do you, if you don't mind me saying so. I love the blazer; there's nothing to beat Saville Row on a man!'

'You can tell?' Howie's thick eyebrows rose in genuine surprise.

'Oh, one can always tell.' Mary glanced down at his large feet. 'Gucci. Very casual and smart with a blazer.'

'Now you've undressed me, how about you?'

'Dressed or undressed?'

'Why not both?'

'Dressed? Charles Svingholm, Undressed? Zilch! Apart from a thong and a touch of Arpège.'

Howie, feeling his heavy cock beginning to swell said hoarsely. 'A drink here before we go to the table?'

'I think from the bulge in your pants we'd better remain seated here until things calm down a bit! And yes, I'd adore a vodka on the rocks.'

There drinks nearly finished, Mary leant forward, saying quietly, 'What is synonymous with all food Italian?'

'Pizza?'

'Exactly! So why not let's make a getaway and make do with a takeaway?' The young woman gave a light laugh. 'I'd better walk closely in front of you so that I am too pointing the way, so to speak! I'll make some excuse. I'm sure the maitre d' is used to a lady changing her mind!'

'My mews house is just around the corner,' said Howie hoarsely, his erection now rampant.

'I know,' said Mary sweetly. 'I know everything about you, Howie Carpenter. After all, I am your employer!' Leaning back against him, she added sotto voce. 'However, what I didn't know was your cock being so enormous! Talk about a fucking fire hydrant!'

'Mary!'

Mary stopped abruptly at the sound of her name, her pert buttocks pressed firmly against Howie's giant erection which in turn had disappeared half way in between the crease of her folds.

'Giles?'

'As ever! What a lovely surprise!'

'Likewise!' Mary gave a high, forced laugh. 'I can't stop to talk Giles but I'll call you tomorrow!'

'I look forward to it!' The dapper art critic's eyes gave a mere flicker as he surveyed the couple standing pressed closely together. He gave a faint smile. 'Ah yes, I can see you have a pressing engagement. Please don't let me keep you!'

CHAPTER 9

'Won't Jeremy and Mark – he's so nosy and always so curious about everything going on even if it has nothing to do with our painting – be curious about a delivery of rugs for the gallery?'

'My dear Francis, they're so up each other's backsides I doubt if they'd even notice the sky should it turn green!' Sybil gave a laugh. 'That's why I've arranged for the rugs to be delivered early Wednesday morning. Franchot never gets here until eleven and Jeremy – now he's ensconced with Mark – is never here before nine. We'll be at the gallery before seven for the delivery. The triumvirate are attending a celebrity party for some tiresome charity – save the snails or something equally as ludicrous! – so I've also arranged for your cheeky-sounding Bob to return at eight the same evening; no earlier. By then the rugs will have be re-rolled and wrapped for their journey to Gay Paree!'

As arranged, Sybil and Francis arrived at the gallery a little before seven to find the van already waiting with the driver, a cheerful young Arab, sitting listening to some weird radio programme while reading one of the more lurid tabloids.

'Miss Sybil!' smiled the young man, giving a smile of hideously stained teeth, 'Good day! Good day!'

'And a good day to you too, Abdul! You have the rugs?'

'Four beautiful rugs! Only the best for you, Miss Sybil! My father, he says only the best for Miss Sybil!'

'And quite right too,' said Sybil, giving the effervescent young man a saccharine smile. 'This way then, Abdul, Mr Francis will help you!'

Once the rugs had been delivered Sybil reached inside his large handbag and, pulling out a wad of cash peeled off a twenty pound note, graciously handing this over to the still smiling young man. 'A small extra thank you, Abdul. You've been most helpful and efficient and I shall be happily telling your father so.'

'May the blessings of Allah be upon you, Miss Sybil!'

'And may my bank manager bless *you*!' smiled Sybil.

Within a short space of time eight so-called Franchot Seatons, carefully covered with protective sheeting, had been rolled up inside their respective rugs and covered with a burlap wrapping.

'Glorious rugs, Sybil,' Francis had observed.

'Well, my dear, as we are going to be using them for a while in the Paris flat, why not another small investment? Besides, cheap is *never* cheerful!'

On the stroke of seven that evening, the rugs were collected by Bob, a swaggering, cheerful, loutish young man who had met Francis before at college. As well as doing independent deliveries – France being a regular run for the purchase of cheap wines – Bob was also employed as a part-time janitor and enjoyed the dubious status of being the local gay stud for 'all those prissy artistic little queens,' as he laughingly boasted to Furlong Fred, his best mate. Bob's formidable 'paint brush' – according to Francis – was more 'industrial,' than for the 'refined canvas!'

'And it's the two of you going to be living there?' The young lout's amusement was obvious. 'Like, together?'

'Oh yes indeed, Mr Trucker Fucker!' said Sybil prissily, taking Francis firmly by the arm and turning to re-enter the gallery. 'My husband and I!'

'Christ!' Bob muttered, slowly making his way out of the cul-de-sac and into Lots Road before taking the motorway for Folkstone and the ferry. 'Now I've really seen it all! 'I've heard of grab a granny but a granny granddad? That must be a fucking first!'

'Did you see his face?' chortled Francis as he and Sybil sat having a much needed glass of wine.

'Unfortunately, dear, I did!' Sybil took a large swallow. 'And if he's the college stud then I'm Marilyn Monroe!'

'How are the team doing?' Jeremy, giving his most ingratiating smile looked questioningly at Sybil and Francis, each concentrating diligently on the large stretched canvas standing in front of them on their respective easels.

'Like Stephenson's rocket,' said Sybil with a small, tight smile, swilling his brush round in a jar of cloudy turps. 'Or, to bring us more up to date, a jet engine!'

'I think rocket sounds more twenty first century!' laughed Francis.

'You would, wouldn't you?' said Jeremy, his mouth twitching, his resentment at the young man's presence apparent.

'Though some people would consider rocket a salad!' cut in Sybil, squeezing a large dollop of yellow paint onto his clean brush.

'Or even a Rockette!' laughed Francis, delighting in their dual baiting of Jeremy.

'Or even a Rockette?' grimaced Jeremy. 'How bizarre that you could reduce something special to the same ranks as that of a mere chorus girl.'

'Now, now, you two!' cut in Sybil, a definite undertone to his gaiety. Turning and gazing imperiously up at Jeremy, he suddenly snapped. 'And you, Jeremy, should remember *not* to bite the *hands* that feed you – and so wholesomely if I may be so old and bold to say!'

'I must say the paintings are all great,' said Jeremy placatingly. 'Simply great!' Giving a further smile, more supercilious than ingratiating, he added. 'In fact the best! I really *am* beginning to thinks the counterfeit Seatons are beginning to put their original counterparts to shame.'

'Better not let your partner in crime hear that!'

'Only for the ears of my partner in *mime*!' said Jeremy glibly.

'Oh, very droll, Jeremy!' said Sybil, flicking another impressive splatter of yellow onto his canvas.

'And this is…?' Jeremy nodded at the large square of canvas in front of his uncle.

'Galaxy Nine. Part of a set of twelve. These are the ones for Sydney.'

'And Abu Dhabi?'

'Already completed and stacked over there.'

'*Brilliant,* Sybil *and* Francis! I really mean it!'

'Why, *thank* you Jeremy! And I do believe you actually do mean it! See how easy it is to be *genuine* at times? Now, if you've seen enough to put your anxious mind at rest, off with you! Boy wonder and I here have several more of these unsavoury doppelgängers to conjure up!'

'Your wishes are my command, Seatons Two and Three!'

'And Jeremy, before you turn tail and run, don't forget this talented twosome are off to France tomorrow.'

'I hadn't forgotten. In fact, that's the other reason I called by.' He reached for an envelope inside his jacket. 'Here's five thousand Euros for you to blow! You both deserve it!' Jeremy's smile, genuine this time, grew even wider at the stunned looks on the two faces. 'I take it the hotel will be put on a company card? Where are you staying? The Ritz? The Crillion? The Georges Cinq?'

'Oh *no*, dear! That would never do!' Sybil looked genuinely shocked. 'I mean, we haven't even *started* the Five Five Five tour as yet and we may need all our reserves for that! No, Francis and I will be staying with an old school friend, Christopher Gregory, who owns a small shop in Montmartre which specialises in rare books.' Avoiding Francis's mischievous grin, he couldn't help but embroider his story even further. 'Dear Christopher, so like his books. Musty, dusty but very sweet! So, that's where we'll be, somewhere mouldy in Montmartre but still mobilised!'

'Still mobilised?'

'On the *mobile,* dear!'

'But of course, how silly of me...' Jeremy gave a self-deprecating laugh. 'Mobilised or immobilised, I promise not to disturb you. Have fun!' With a wave of his arm he turned and left thinking, Christ, what a set up! One old queen along with Miss Priscilla, little queen for the desert! *Not* my idea of a fun weekend break at all!

Entering the office he found Mark checking through a list of notes. Mark looked up with a smile. 'Everything OK with Mother Bread and Baby Butter?'

'As innocent as the Babes in the Wood.'

'Poor little dears!'

'Creepy little dears. I mean, if you're going to be gay at least be a *normal* gay!'

'Like us, you mean?'

'Exactly. I mean, what could be more normal than fisting, anal penetration, blow jobs and the occasional golden shower?"

'Precisely!' Mark gave out a hoot of laughter. 'Now, having put my mind at rest as to my obviously very run-of-the-mill proclivities, here's our schedule. All flights are reserved and even though Sybil thought it a gross extravagance that she and the boy also fly First Class – she was quite prepared to do all that flying sitting in steerage, would you believe? – we are all together.'

'How lovely!'

'The paintings are to be shipped off on September first, latest, and we begin our marathon on the thirteenth with Eurostar to Paris early morning, returning that afternoon for our opening here and then the morning flight to New York. Of course you and I will have already been to Paris and to New York for the setting up. We have a full day each to work on the exhibitions in Sydney and Dhabi but, with the relevant wall elevations marked out with which painting goes where, our team out there should have it all one hundred per cent for our arrival. It should only take a quick recce of all on arrival prior to the openings.'

'You've got it all worked out to the final detail, haven't you? Marky,' said Jeremy admiringly.

Mark gave a disparaging grin. 'My part's the easy part! I'm taking it for granted the paintings will be ready in time for shipping out.'

'No problem! Dhabi is done and Sydney almost complete. We're definitely on schedule. So I see no problem apart from out main problem. When and where does the ODing take place?'

'A few weeks after our return. We've got to let the papers have a field day with shots of our Croesus of the Canvas – wait until those sales prices hit the press! – partying and generally behaving badly.'

'And the Babes?'

'I told you I'd come up with a beaut! Ever since seeing *Out of Africa*, Sybil has had a secret yearning to emulate either Karen Blixen or Meryl Streep, or both! I think it's the pith helmet that attracts, more so than lions, lithesome Masai warriors, safaris and all that shit! Well, after sissy boy disappears I shall suggest to the distraught Sybil she take a break somewhere completely different to get over it all. I'll vaguely mention Africa and I'm sure the old thing – distraught or not – will bite!'

'And sissy boy?'

'As I said, he simply disappears. If that's any *cold* comfort to you?'

'You don't mean?'

'Oh yes, I do very much mean!'

'Fan-fucking-tastic!'

'There'll have to be a cooling off period.'

'Even better. Who know? Perhaps once frost bitten, Nic the Nec could become the latest addition to our portfolio!'

'Dare I say it?'

'I'll say it with you!'

'Cool!' they cried in unison.

Across London a similar conversation was taking place.

'I do wish you'd tell me exactly what you have planned,' said Mary petulantly.

'All in good time,' murmured Howie, idly inserting a large, hairy finger into her moist cunt, giving it a twist then pulling it out and holding it to his broad, flat nose. Sniffing deeply he muttered, 'Ah, nectar! Pure nectar!'

'Christ, Howie Carpenter! At times you can be quite revolting!'

'And you love it! C'mon. Two fingers this time and then I'll really fuck you. I'm in a sideways mood!'

'No!' Mary pushed his huge hand aside and, swinging her long legs off the bed, stood up. She glared down at the grinning man who was now sucking lasciviously on his finger. 'Fuck you, Mr Carpenter! I'm getting tired of your games. I'm leaving now and we won't be meeting again until after your return which I certainly trust sees you arriving back here empty handed, if you catch my drift?'

'Empty handed? Very funny, Mary and of course I "catch your drift," and whatever the fuck else you wish.' He nodded in the direction of the bedroom door. 'You know your way out of this stable, I believe?'

Without a word Mary picked up her clothes from a nearby chair and walked calmly out into the small sitting room. Fifteen minutes later, sitting in the nearby Richoux Cafe she made a phone call. 'Our hatchet man seems to be well on his way to becoming a major problem.'

'Calm down, dear,' said the soothing voice of the recipient. 'I've discovered he's booked to Sydney direct and then on to Abu Dhabi. If you deem it necessary, why not make it a three hit wonder as opposed to a two hit which means hatchet man is also made – shall we say – redundant?'

'But what about all the money he's already had?'

'Such a vulgar word, money! But to put your pretty mind to rest, see it as a case of here today, gone tomorrow. That's the joy of computerised transactions. Thanks to our very overpriced hacker, they're not infallible!'

'What are you doing?'

'Speaking to you, my dear!'

'I mean, where *are* you?'

'You?'

'Richoux, South Audley Street.'

'So why not a discreet lunch at The Connaught? Or is it too close to home and we may just be spotted by your Incredible Hulk?'

'You never know with that one! Better to be safe than sorry. Let's meet at San Lorenzo, I know he loathes the place. He once broke a chair there on sitting down and he's never recovered from the humiliation!'

'Sounds perfect. An hour?'

'See you there!'

CHAPTER 10

RUE MICHEL ANGE:

Effusive to begin with but decidedly curious a few minutes later, a smiling Jeanette showed Sybil and Francis her handiwork.

'It's lovely, dear,' chirruped Sybil, '*Tres bon! Tres tres chic*!' he cried as a sniggering Francis, as if developing sudden a sneezing fit, simply buried his face in his hands. He looked at the simple room, modestly but stylishly furnished with a comfortable sofa, two side tables with lamps, a low, modern coffee table, two bergere-style chairs and a small dinette set. The four wrapped rolls delivered by Bob had been left in the bedroom which boasted a large bed, two side tables, a pair of lamps, two small upright chairs and nothing more. 'Oh!' he exclaimed looking across at the small dining table. 'Flowers! How lovely. What are they Jeanette? I take it I may call you Jeanette? Madam la Concierge sounds so formal, doesn't it?'

'Jeanette will be fine,' replied the smiling woman in perfect, accented English. 'Roses, madam.'

'Roses?'

'The flowers, madam.'

'Oh, so they are and they too are *tres, tres chic*! Now, dear Jeanette, if you would very kindly leave my son and I to get the feel of the *maison,* we'd be ever so grateful! We'll be leaving on Sunday evening so we won't need to bother you at all. Thank you *so* much for all you've done. *Merci beacoups* and *au revoir*!'

'Do you have to be such an old *camp*?' shrieked Francis, doubling up with laughter on the sofa.

'Would you have me any other way?' carolled Sybil pirouetting into the small kitchenette and opening the fridge. 'Dear Gregory has done us proud. Oodles of Chablis and yes, I do believe a bottle of bubbly! What else? Eggs, milk and some ham? That must be Jeanette. Foie Gras and some smoked salmon? That's obviously Gregory. Who ever said a disgraced priest's life is not an abundant one!' He turned back to a still grinning Francis. 'Now dear, do something to earn your sordid keep! There should be some glasses in one of these cupboards so Francis, precious, would you do the honours whilst I slip into something incredibly vulgar and then we're going to hit this old town for a bit of ooh la la!'

Holding their wine glasses brimming with the sparkling liquid the two stood on the small balcony looking down at the busy street, several floors below.

'It's fab, Sybil,' breathed Francis. 'Utterly, utterly fab. Like you!'

'Why, thank you dear, but change that to *we're* fab.' Sybil gestured to the four rolls of rugs now brought through to the sitting room. 'We'll deal with those later. Jean Claude will be here at nine o'clock tomorrow. He's our lord and master's contact here in Paris.'

'Will I ever get to meet our mysterious lord and master?'

'All in good time, Francis precious; all in good time and preferably in Cape Town where we all will eventually convene.'

'Monsieur Jean Claude?'

'*Oui, Madam*! I am so pleased to meet you at long last!'

'Oh, my' whispered Sybil.

Hercules meets Sex on Legs! Thought Francis, his curled up little cock giving a tiny tremor.

'Do come in,' trilled Sybil, regaining his composure.

'Yes, do come in!' echoed Francis.

The big man walked confidently into the small room filling it not only with his size but with his powerful male presence. 'I tried to make it as comfortable as possible for you but I was also told you may be doing some more decorating later? Maybe I can again offer my help?' Jean Claude smiled, showing a set of dazzling white teeth, offset by his deep tan and further enhanced by a pair of sparkling blue eyes. A thick cap of glossy, dark wavy hair completed the god-like effigy. 'I was asked to make sure you had the basic necessities,' – he gestured around the room – 'such as seating and next door, a bed!' He gave another brilliant smile. 'I trust you found it comfortable?'

'Very, thank you, Jean Claude!' said Sybil crisply, as if talking to an errant schoolboy.

'I kept the furnishings simple, but perhaps you may wish to change these at a later date? I asked the concierge to supply bread, milk, some eggs and some fruit but she tells me another gentleman – a priest – has also, as you English say, "stocked you up!"'

'Ah yes, dear Father Gregory, a friend of my brother. Dear David – such a sweet, considerate *sib*-ling – must have asked him to do the tiny favour!' Sybil put a small hand to his fashionable Mulberry blouse. 'Oh, Jean Claude! Forgive me! How rude! How remiss of me. Would you care for a libation of sorts? Coffee? I know it's early but, as we English also say, "it's never *too* early." We finished the champagne last night but we do have some delicious chilled Chablis!'

'That would be most agreeable, Madam Sybil.' Jean Claude gave another show of perfect teeth before pointing to the four rolled up packages. 'And while you get the wine, may I?'

'But of course, and Francis will help you.'

Moving the small coffee table to make more room Jean Claude, aided by the overwhelmed Francis expertly opened up and unrolled the first rug. Once this was laid out flat he carefully lifted the first of the protective sheets to reveal the top one of the two enclosed canvases.

'Fantastic!' he breathed. 'Marvellous!' He turned to Sybil, now standing with a tray and three glasses of wine. 'I have seen Franchot Seaton's work in photographs, but to see these like this, *alive,* is more than wonderful. It's exceptional!'

'From such enthusiasm we take it these first eight meet with your approval,' said Sybil impishly. A statement, not a question.

'Oh yes, Madam Sybil, Jean Claude likes them very much.' He nodded at the other three rolls. 'I feel that if the quality of the second here and the remaining six over there are any match to this one, even a remote match, there is no need to unroll them here.'

'They're all as good as, I can assure you.'

'Madam Sybil, Monsieur Francis. I salute you! I have heard of your skills. In fact, I know these are your works, not Franchot Seaton's! I was told of your skills and I must agree the two of you have been remarkable.' He took a slim-line phone from the inner pocket of his suede jacket. 'I have a van downstairs with two men waiting to be summonsed. May I?'

'Please, Jean.'

'And Madam, in anticipation of our delight I brought a case of Dom Perignon as a thank you but,' and here the handsome man gave a deep chuckle, 'I feel sure not even a case of the finest champagne can compete with this!' Reaching into his pocket once more he withdrew a thin envelope. 'Confirmation of your cash transfer, Madam Sybil. The money will be in your account by midmorning.'

'Even better!' exclaimed a beaming Sybil. 'And even though it may be warm, why not a celebratory glass of champagne when your man brings the case up?'

'An excellent idea, Madam Sybil!' Jean Claude nodded at the sound of a discreet knocking on the door. 'The champagne arrives!' He gave both Sybil and the still mesmerised Francis another of his dazzling smiles. Striding to the door he pulled this open to reveal two grinning men dressed in overalls, one bearing a tray holding an ice bucket with a chilled bottle of champagne plus three flutes, the other a case held in his brawny arms. 'Let it never be said, Madam Sybil, that a true Frenchman would offer a lady warm champagne!'

'Oh my,' whispered Sybil, almost lost for words.

'Wow!' said Francis.

'Allow me,' said Jean Claude taking the glistening bottle from out of the ice.

The rugs safely taken down to the van, Jean Claude sat with Sybil and Francis, finishing the bottle of champagne. The charming Frenchman, aware of Francis's surreptitious glances couldn't help smiling to himself. Yes, my sweet – or 'precious' as this funny old drag auntie calls you – you are certainly both and perhaps even more! His moment came when Sybil excused himself saying daintily he required 'a visit to the ladies' room.'

'Francis,' said Jean Claude softly.

'Yes, Jean Claude?' Francis looked up adoringly at the dark-haired French version of Daniel Craig.

'You have a mobile?'

'Yes!'

'Give me your number! Quickly, my *ange*, before the old man returns!'

'Ohmigod!'

'*Vit, mon cher*!' Jean Claude punched in the appropriate numbers, managing to return his mobile to his pocket just as Sybil re-entered the room.

'I must really be going,' the Frenchman said, having already politely stood on Sybil's return.

'It's been a pleasure, Jean Claude,' smiled Sybil.

'Miss Sybil, I understand you have a meeting *á deux* with the Professor at six o'clock?'

'On the dot!'

'And Monsieur Francis is joining you?'

'Jean Claude, even the closest of friends have to sometimes take a back seat.' Sybil gave a light, teasing laugh. 'So feel free to call Francis on his mobile or, better still, invite him out now! These walls in these conversions are so indiscreet, are they not?'

Jean Claude and Francis burst out laughing.

'Does *nothing* escape you, Sybil?'

'Only Jean Claude, it seems!' said Sybil glibly. 'Have fun, my dears. I will more than likely have dinner with the Professor so why not make yourselves at home back here? There's plenty of champagne, so what more could you wish for?' The latter comment was said with a mischievous little smile.

'I love you Sybil!' cried Francis, rushing across and giving the elderly man a hug.

'And I love you too, precious!' Looking over Francis's shoulder to the broadly smiling Frenchman, he added. 'Take care of my precious, Jean Claude.'

'It will be an honour,' said the man, a lump rising in his throat at the true affection he was privy to witnessing. At the same time he could not but help the feeling of another sensation, one of impending dread.

CAMBON BAR, RITZ HOTEL:

'Sybil!'

'Professor!'

'Oh, my teasing darling, how I loathe it so when you call me that!' Giles Delaware gave Sybil a light kiss on his heavily rouged cheek. 'My, my,' he said, holding her back and looking adoringly. 'Just look at you, my muse, my perfection!'

'Oh, wicked, wicked Giles! Don't! You know what happens when you start smooth talking me in those *sibilant* tones!'

'God, Sybs! What a ghastly pun, if intended!'

'It was, wasn't it,' giggled Sybil. 'God, and I was beginning to think I couldn't get any worse!'

'You, my dear, like a vintage wine, can only improve!'

'Backhanded flatterer!'

'Exquisiteness!'

'Dear Giles.' Sybil, taking a dainty sip of his Martini, looked endearingly at the smiling dapper, white-haired man sitting opposite. 'Who would have thought…?'

'Tell me! Giles Delaware, lothario supreme and well-known lady killer, deeply, madly, hopelessly and extravagantly in love with a transvestite!'

'Professor!'

'Transvestite!'

'Oh, how I love it when you tease me, my *peit chou*!'

'*Petit chou*? I thought I was more your rooster!'

'Rooster then!'

'Adorable!' Giles lent forward. 'May I suggest we do the proper thing and discuss our bit of business here where there are no er... *major* distractions and later, I've ordered a discreet – or hopefully – deliciously indiscreet supper up in my suite.'

'You devil you!'

'If only I had a pair of rampant horns instead of only one, my darling Jezebel!'

'I can assure you, Giles darling, your one horn is more than efficient, unlike this one Martini!'

'Point taken!' said Giles, resulting in the two of them bursting into a series of giggles. Martinis ordered and a sense of decorum re-established, the art critic's face took on a more serious demeanour. 'Right, I take it Jean Claude was his usual reliable, impeccable self?'

'That glorious man couldn't have done more! Charming, efficient and, if I'm not mistaken, blissfully fucking the boy wonder as we speak!'

'Good! I was rather hoping that would be the case. Keeps it all as one happy family.'

'He's not going to hurt young Francis is he? I couldn't allow that.'

'Sybs, I can assure you Jean Claude is a hundred per cent honourable to the point of embarrassment.' Giles lowered his voice conspiratorially, 'He was married but it was a disaster. I've known the young man for some time and always thought he was *that way inclined* but like so many of those poor, tortured souls he battled so strongly against his true feelings. And his family, typical wealthy French *bourgeoisie,* would have not been at all understanding. A small – shall we say experimental – dalliance *after* the wedding led to an immediate separation followed by an unpleasant divorce. Even worse, Jean Claude went on to discover the young man reciprocating his desires was not a student at the Sorbonne but a highly successful *poule de luxe* – a high class rent boy in other words. Since getting his willy – it's enormous so I'm told! – well and truly er... burned, he's been avoiding the world of romance. How intriguing that your Francis may now be changing that! But enough about the love birds to be – we can but hope – and back to the paintings.'

'Eight delivered today and another eight in a couple of weeks' time, literally before we leave for the States. We're working on these now. What nephew Jeremy viewed a few days ago were not the ones for Australia which, like those for Abu Dhabi, are all completed. That young man has his head so in the clouds at the moment – he and that Mark are really up to something – that I swear if his balls weren't in a bag he'd leave them behind one morning!.

'So elegant, my divine Sybs!'

'Of course, and with Jeremy and that dreadful Franchot out of the picture – oh dear, we *are* in for an evening of puns, it seems! – I inherit all of Spiers-Seaton and the rest! Not only will *we,* dear Giles, therefore hold claim to all the unsold works in the public eye but then also to the forty odd – surprise, surprise – unknown works which have never been seen. The world's our oyster, *including* a very big pearl!'

'You really dislike nephew Jeremy, don't you Sybil?'

'He killed *my* Sybil,' said David Spiers simply. 'And what goes round, comes around. End of story.' He took another sip of his drink. 'I deserve a fucking Oscar, Golden Globe – you name it – for the performance I've been giving over these past years.'

The attraction between Giles and Sybil at the luncheon hosted by Jeremy and Tone at Bellamy's, had been immediate. Giles, his reputation as a ladies man almost legendary, had inadvertently found himself deeply fascinated by the world of transvestism, though not in the practice itself but by those involved. Though not a participant he revelled in his clandestine Thursday visits to Ted's Place, a popular 'trannies' venue in South London, a decided contrast to his usual high profile social life.

Sybil had proved to be the answer to all his fantasies. Giles had found him highly intelligent, amusing and extraordinarily attractive. Desperate to make contact again he had been shrewd enough to wait until after the gallery opening. It was the following day he took the plunge.

Telephoning Spiers-Seaton Fine Arts he had casually asked to be put through to their *directrice*. Jeremy, coping with both a hangover and the constantly ringing phones (their secretary had not shown up that morning) and not paying much attention to the strange falsetto voice being used, had simply put him through to Sybil in the studio.

'Miss Sybil speaking.'

'Miss Sybil, Giles Delaware.'

There was a moment's silence. 'The art critic?'

'The one and only Miss Sybil and may I come straight to the point?'

'It depends how sharp your point is!'

'Oh, Miss Sybs! Sorry, Miss Sybil. You were magic at Bellamy's, enchanting last night and sound too, too delicious today! Have dinner with me tonight?'

'Dinner?' Oh, Mr Delaware, I somehow think you may have got your wires crossed, this is Sybil Spiers, *Directrice* of Spiers-Seaton Fine Arts you're speaking to!'

'I very much like the sound of our wires crossing, Miss Sybs! I know you're a *man* after my own heart so what *do* you say to dinner *á deux* at The Ivy followed by a plethora of electrifying shocks with our wires crossing later?'

'Oh my!'

'Not "oh my," Miss Sybs! Oh *yes*!'

'I'd be enchanted, even more so – if that were ever possible – if you would deign to do a slow, slow strip and deliciously tease me, my dear,' murmured Giles later as he lay back against the damask-covered sofa in the drawing room of his elegant Eaton Square flat.

'I do a really mean, sexy strip to *anything* by Shirley Bassey,' said Sybil loftily – and slightly drunkenly – standing legs akimbo, a large glass of crème de menthe in his one hand. 'Do you *have* any Shirley Bassey?'

'Show me a bon vivant who *doesn't* own any Shirley Bassey and I'll show you a fraud! So which of the Dame's delicious renditions would you be prepared to strip and tease to?'

'*Big Spender*!'

'Why am I not surprised?'

As Shirley Bassey's enthralling, powerful voice reverberated around the lofty room, Sybil began. Bumping and grinding, twisting and turning plus flinging his arms outstretched in a perfect parody of the legend's extravagant gestures and miming the words, Sybil first took off his heavy faux pearl bracelet (Chanel), followed by a long string necklace, again of faux pearls and again by Chanel. Next came the Chanel jacket followed by the Chanel skirt leaving the skeletal-like Sybil standing in a pair of stilettos, tights and a silk blouse. Off came the blouse to reveal a pert, lacy bra. '*Hey, sweet falsies!*' warbled Sybil, '*Fal-si-fy a bit for me!*'

Giles, eyes wide, found the performance unbelievably arousing, so much so that by the end of the number he too was standing, buck naked, a bright, pink slightly paunchy figure with what Sibyl would later recall, 'An erect prick so enormous that I thought he'd over balance!'

'My Sybs! My Sybs!' Giles groaned and moaned as he gallantly mounted him, having first slyly asked which position Sybil would prefer.

Sybil's reply had been succinct. 'Chanel owned a poodle, didn't she? So we'll do it doggie fashion!'

A few months later Giles introduced his new paramour to a Miss Tiffany Cowper. 'This could be interesting,' said Giles. 'Tiffany Cowper firmly believes your Jeremy and that Seaton fellow murdered her parents.'

By this stage Giles had been made aware of Sybil's major contribution to the Franchot Seaton machine and the counterfeiting taking place. After meeting up with Tiffany, Operation Scupper – a name chosen by pure coincidence – was duly formed.

CHAPTER 11

'How was Gay Paree?'

'Very French and not at all that gay, thank you, Jeremy!'

'Oh, and that's it?'

'Jeremy dear, you're not all interested in what Francis and I got up to, so let's leave it, please!' Seeing a flash of annoyance cross Jeremy's face, Sybil added, 'What does one do in Paris anyway? We did what most tourists do – it was Francis's first visit after all – went sightseeing! I must say the Louvre can be quite, quite exhausting.'

'No Franchot Seatons there as yet, I take it?' said Jeremy with a light laugh.

'Oh Jeremy, what an outrageous thing to suggest, even in jest! Imagine the poor Mona Lisa's expression, changing from one of constipation to that of total enema!'

'Surely you mean enigma? I don't quite get the enema reference?'

'Enema, Jeremy, enema – the shock of being introduced to some serious shit!'

Jeremy gave a mirthless laugh. 'I must say you do talk in the most ridiculous riddles at times, Sybil. Quite irritating, if you really want know.'

''I don't "really want to know" and now dear, duty calls! Back to the brushstroke as we artists say.'

'Francis?'

'Jean Claude! What a wonderful surprise!'

'I miss you, my darling. My soul misses you and my pee pee misses you!'

'Oh, and how I miss *you*, Jean Claude!' Francis, his voice choked, adding, 'I can't believe I have to wait a whole four days before we meet again!'

'A weekend together is better than no time together but, as I said to Miss Sybil, I wish there was arrangement we could sort out – I want you here in Paris…'

'I want to be in Paris!' cut in Francis. 'I *have* to be in Paris with you!'

'I know, I know, my darling, but as Miss Sybil says, we must be patient.' Jean Claude cleared his throat. 'You are fully aware of our plans, the Professor's plans, *non*?'

'Of course *I'm aware*! I'm aware of everything!'

'That we all meet up in Cape Town?'

'Of course!' Francis's voice had now become petulant.

'So, my sweet, you see we simply do have to be patient and mark – ha! – time until we all meet out there. However you will be here for the weekend and I the following weekend I shall be visiting you in London. I will be staying with the Professor at Eaton Square and he, like your true love here, looks forward to yet another guest, you!'

'Giles Delaware! I just knew it! Of course *he's* the Professor!' Francis gave a whoop of laughter, his former sulk evaporating. 'How could I have been so blind when it's been staring me in the face!'

'What is? What has?'

'Giles and Sybil, they're lovers and of course he's the professor she's always referring to when not referring to Giles Delaware, the art critic!'

Jean Claude gave a whistle of amazement. 'They are?'

'Oh yes, Jean Claude, they most certainly are. And I think it all happened over a lunch!' Francis gave a snigger. 'Apparently he possesses the biggest willy in history – or that's the rumour here amongst London's higher echelon!'

'Willy? What is this willy?'

'Cock, Jean Claude. Pee pee!'

'Ah, so you don't think your Jean Claude's pee pee – this willy thing – big enough for you, my darling?'

'Jean Claude, if your pee pee, willy, cock or whatever, was any bigger, my voice would sound as it were in an echo chamber!'

'So the size of my pee pee, willy, cock is OK?'

'Doubly OK, Jean Claude!'

'Thank God for big mercies! So, my darling, you continue with your painting, take care of Miss Sybil and I will be waiting for you at Gard du Nord on Friday.'

'I'll be wearing a green carnation!'

'*Pardon*?'

'English for a big smile!'

SYDNEY, AUSTRALIA:

'Nev? Howie!'

'Howie! How the devil are ya mate?'

Howie grimaced at the loud Australian twang coming over the static.

'Great, thanks. And you, Nev?'

'Even greater knowin' yer goin' ta be here in two weeks time!'

'That's why I'm ringing. Major change in plan, Nev, and I need to talk you seriously, fucking seriously, my old friend! As I've never been to your neck of the woods before I thought I'd bring myself out a few days earlier, like tomorrow! As I've said, we've got some serious talking to do and arrangements to make.'

'Take it as done. I've got you booked at the Park Hyatt but will bring your reservation forward.' Nev lowered his voice conspiratorially, 'You want privacy, great! Gives me a good excuse for me to get away for a few days from the missus! She's acting a right, tight cunt at the moment! Got her fuckin' ma staying for what I think could be a fuckin' eternity. Apparently old Lucifer doesn't want the meddlesome old cunt at his party!' Nev's loud guffaw ending in a hacking, coughing fit during which Howie held on patiently.

'Jesus, Howie! I thought I was a gonner there for a sec! No, mate, you get your arse on Quantas and I'll show you the time of your life!'

'The time of your life,' saw Nev – their complicated business plans having been meticulously made and therefore ready to be implemented – taking Howie on an illicit trip to 'shoot some 'roos instead of fuckin' Abbos! *And* you'll be seeing part of the outback where even that Crocodile Dundee arsehole would shit his pants! Not a civilised human so to speak – apart from us two fellas! – for miles!'

Unfortunately for Howie – or at least according to the details finally filtered back to England – on being 'caught short' in the bush and squatting down for an uncontrollable shit, the big man had unknowingly squatted atop a well-camouflaged snake, an Inland Taipan, Australia's most deadly. Within half an hour a tearful Nev confirmed Howie as dead.

Later, when regularly regaling the episode to a group of alarmed but fascinated tourists buying him continuous rounds of drinks in a King's Cross Bar, Nev always ended by saying, 'what a waste, what a fuckin' waste!' Cracking into a smile he gave a great bellow of laughter. 'Waste! Shit! Geddit?'

Howie's earlier departure from London had gone unnoticed. Tiffany, aka Mary Magdalene, having announced there would be no further contact until after his return from the so-called business trip, simply put the lack of communication down to Howie indulging in a major sulk.

A further complication or twist to the tale had been an accidental meeting between Tiffany and Tone which had taken place at a party given by a well-known film director. Having never met Franchot

Seaton, the artist, the young woman was dismayed to find the man not only handsome and devastatingly charming, but highly amusing and intelligent or, as the director's wife had put it, 'totally charismatic!'

'Such a pity I'm part of a plan to kill you!' she kept murmuring to herself. 'You're quite, quite divine! I can now see what they mean when by the song *That Old Black Magic*!' Accepting a glass of champagne from the ever attentive Tone –the attraction had been mutual – she had given the smiling man a warm smile in return thinking, Oh, what the fuck! Some you win, some you lose while you, my black Adonis, murdered my mum and dad.

Tone, having no reason to even remotely connect the name Tiffany with the couple he and Jeremy had so cruelly killed – her name may have been mentioned in any earlier conversations but it had never registered, Jeremy only ever foul mouthing the husband and wife – found the sudden change in the young woman's friendliness towards him confusing.

'Have I said something wrong?' he asked worriedly as she handed back her half-empty glass with a barely audible, 'I must go.'

'Sadly not said,' came the mumbled reply which only added to his puzzlement. Oh, what the hell, Tiffany thought. If he's as gorgeous in bed as he is out of it, why *not* torture him a bit, maybe even fuck him? Now, that would be a sweet revenge! She shook herself out of her reverie. 'I apologise. It's simply I've got a bit of a sudden headache plus the heat and the noise in here is not helping.'

'Would a bit of fresh air help?' came the concerned reply, 'There's quite a bit of a garden out the back.'

'Why not?'

Two hours later the elegant couple were sitting in San Lorenzo, the glamorous Knightsbridge eatery, oblivious to the stares and whispers of the other diners.

'Have you ever been with a black man?' Tone's sudden question coming out of the blue as they sat smiling comfortably at each other over their large glasses of grappa.

'No, I must say the opportunity has never arisen!' Tiffany gave a playful smile. 'But there's always a first time, isn't there?'

'There is!' said Tone with a grin. 'We could always go back to my studio but I must warn you I have two house mates.'

And don't I know it, thought Tiffany. Sybil and Francis!

'I think,' she whispered, leaning closer across the small table, 'as it *will* be my first time with a black man – and a gorgeous one at that! – I'd feel much more comfortable in my own bed and, apart from a very possessive cat, I do live alone!'

'Anywhere near here?'

'Cadogan Square,' said Tiffany. 'About five minutes walk away.'

Looking at the spread-eagled, sleeping Tone as daybreak began to filter through the muslin blinds of her bedroom, Tiffany could not help but emitting a small, sad sigh. 'What a waste,' she murmured, unaware that on the other side of the world a similar observation was simultaneously being made.

'Do I see you again?' asked Tone, eyeing the gorgeous girl across his mug of coffee.

'I don't think so,' said Tiffany with a small, almost wistful smile. 'From what I'm told you're off to Paris tomorrow than back here tomorrow night for your big exhibition opening and then on to New York the following day followed by Australia and more!' She gave a rueful grin. 'I do read the papers, Mr Franchot Seaton, artist extraordinaire!' She shook her long dark hair, 'So no, I don't think so.'

'If I may, I'd like to call you everyday while I'm away.'

'Feel free to do so, but you're only a way five or six days...'

'Could seem an eternity,' laughed Tone.

'Many a word spoken in jest...' began Tiffany sadly, the unfinished words left hanging.

CHAPTER 12

'On your marks – geddit? – get set, and here we go!'

As the sleek 6.55 a.m. Eurostar train pulled out of St Pancras International bound for Paris Gare du Nord, Jeremy skilfully opened the bottle of iced champagne, grinning effusively at a smiling Mark, a sullen-looking Tone, an excited Francis and a chirpy Sybil. Having handed over the filled flutes he raised and, with a voice filled with genuine emotion, spoke the words which, or the next few days, would capture the hearts of the ever hungry press. 'Five! Five! Five!'

'Five! Five! Five!' chorused the other four faces with even Tone seeming to catch the mood at last.

'You'll come *alive* with Five! Five! Five!' Sybil's sing song rhyme being greeted with loud cheers.

'Spiers – Seaton, never beaten!' cried Tone.

'Were in the money!' chanted Mark.

'Money makes the world go round!' sang Jeremy.

'I love Paris!' crooned Francis.

Thanks to Mark there had been several photographers at the station to catch the group boarding their Premier Class coach before leaving. An even larger number had been alerted for their 10.17 a.m. arrival in Paris.

Much to the group's delight there was even a photographer accompanying them on their journey, a charming red-headed Scot named Jamie, who, as he kept reminding them in his broad Scottish accent, was there to record the momentous occasion for 'posterity!.'

'For posterity!' cried the five, laughingly mimicking Jamie.

The cheerful mood continued unabated for the full length of the journey with the five arriving, with Jamie still in tow, at the gallery a good hour and a half before the opening of the exhibition. Jeremy and Mark, as previously arranged, had visited the gallery two days before in order to make sure that the set up was, to use his words, 'Shit hot!'

To the delight of the group a surprise visitor waiting for them in the reception to the gallery was their own Giles Delaware.

'Giles!' Cried Jeremy, genuinely thrown. 'What a wonderful surprise! What an honour!'

'Well, you didn't think for a miniscule second I'd miss the start of your *Modern Master Marathon*, did you? After all, and even though I say it myself, I *was* the one firing the starter's pistol!'

'You're right, Giles! Absolutely right! And thank you, thank you' – Jeremy was still pumping the bemused man's hand enthusiastically – 'thank you for being here. It really *is* the icing on the cake!'

'You never told me you would be here!' hissed a delighted Sybil when he and Giles had finally managed a few snatched moments together.

'Simply looking after my glorious goose who has been kept so busy laying all those golden eggs for us,' laughed Giles. Nodding in Jeremy's direction he added, 'He loves it all, doesn't he?'

'Well, he'd better make hay while the sun shines!' muttered Sybil. 'Rather like your appearance here, he has another surprise guest awaiting him in Sydney, Father Time.'

The evening exhibition back in London was equally as successful with Giles again present, having journeyed back with the five and a very drunken Jamie.

'I didn't see much of young Francis at the exhibition this morning,' Giles had casually remarked to Sybil. 'In fact I only noticed him on the journey back.'

'Ah, but you can bet your last Euro Jean Claude did!'

'Another sell out!' beamed Mark cutting into their conversation. As with Paris, the whole London collection had been sold within the first half hour.

'Just as well you've had Franchot on so tight a leash recently,' said Giles glibly. 'Rumour also has it there is a stash of Franchot Seatons lurking.'

'Rumours, Giles, rumours!' interrupted Jeremy, who, unnoticed, had joined the three. 'It'll be a case of the old slave syndrome all over again when we get back!' he laughed, casting a meaningful in the direction of Tone surrounded by a clutch of admirers.

Later the following evening, the five found themselves sitting exhausted in Jeremy and Mark's de luxe suite in exclusive Peninsula Hotel on Fifth Avenue. Even though they were all worn out there was a feeling of euphoria amongst the group although Sybil had been aware of Tone's almost subdued and, at times, distracted mood. On several occasions he had left the others to use the telephone in the bedroom. 'One of my other business calls to London,' as he vaguely put it. To his acute dismay the telephone number given to him by Tiffany kept going to voice mail.

'So, are we on to something good here, Marky?' said Jeremy, his face turning again to a scowl as Tone once more bounded to his feet and left the room. 'Chirst!' said Jeremy to nobody in particular. 'Talk about a prick caught in a hot shower! What the fuck's the matter with him? This is *his* night! He's got the whole of New York's finest eating out of his hand and he doesn't appear to give a shit!'

'Maybe he's in love,' said Mark sarcastically, pouring himself a large brandy.

'Marky,' said Jeremy wearily as he reached for the brandy balloon proffered by his lover, 'Tone Seaton has been strictly faithful to himself since day one. Love? He doesn't even *begin* to know the meaning of the word!'

'And you, I take it Jeremy, are an expert on the subject?' This from a tight-lipped Sybil. He nodded at Jeremy's drink. '*And* whilst you're at it Mark, yes please, I'd also like another brandy as would perhaps young Francis.' He gave both young men a steely look. 'After all, we've got to keep these counterfeiting fingers well *oiled*, haven't we?'

'Bitch!'

'I heard that Jeremy, dear!' said Sybil softly. 'However, do try and behave – perhaps even be pleasant for the next three days – even if the effort kills you!'

I just hope this Mr Carpenter is as good as Giles professes,' said Sybil to Francis back in the privacy of their suite (for once not catching a probable pun). 'I don't think I can take Jeremy's arrogance and lack of consideration for anyone and everything much longer.'

'Calm, Sybil, calm.' An anxious Francis gave the old man a gentle kiss, his lips coming away covered in Sybil's overnight rejuvenating cream. 'You've managed to hold yourself together for all this length of time so, take these three or four last days in your stride.'

'One cannot *stride* in stilettos!' said Sybil, a small grin finally appearing on his tired face.

'That's my old harridan!' laughed Francis. 'Atta girl!'

SYDNEY:

'God, what a haul but what a view!' Jeremy stood on the balcony looking out across the famous Sydney Harbour with its views of the hooded opera house and the spectacular arched bridge. 'I feel spaced out, man,' he added, giving Mark a high five, 'Wild and spaced out.'

'So you should, Jer. This reception at Preston-Palin this evening is going to make New York seem small fry. I mean the press here are already billing Tone as *The Wizard of Aus*! For Christ's sake!'

'Some fucking wizard!' snapped Jeremy ignoring Mark's good news and considering the bad. 'Talk about a black mood! He's the fucking Black Hole!'

'He drunkenly confessed on the flight here that he's got the hots for some bird back in London.'

'Who? Some fucking little flooise? Some groupie?'

'No. some bird with a strange name, something to do with jewellery. Emerald? Diamond? Emerald maybe?'

'He would go for a fucking emerald, wouldn't he being the fucking wizard of Aus?'

'I don't get it?'

'The Emerald City in *The Wizard of Oz*, Marky' Jeremy gave a look of mock exasperation. 'Surely as a one hundred per cent bona fide pink gay you should know your Judy Garland!'

Sybil's phone call to Giles on a non-traceable mobile was one of growing anxiety. 'We're here getting prepared for tonight's event but, as yet, I haven't heard a word from your contact.'

'What?' Giles's concern was manifest. 'No message *at all*?'

'Nothing, dearest. Zilch!'

'Damn! He was meant to have left you – as I told you – a coded message from "Alice" saying "Hope Springs Eternal! Salvation is Nigh," simply to confirm all is in place. Christ!' Giles's voice came worriedly over the crackling line. 'He's only got tomorrow to deal with Franchot and then a distraught Jeremy keeping "a stiff upper lip" in Dhabi!'

'I have a bad feeling about this Giles.'

'I'd much prefer you to be feeling *me,* my dearest! Don't worry your perfect little head about it. Get your Francis to give you a back rub and think delicious dastardly thoughts about your Giles while he has a long distance wank!'

'You're not!'

'I most certainly am and if I am n-o-t m-i-s-t-a-k-e-n I-m j-u-s-t a-b-o-u-t t-o aah c-o-m-e!'

'Really, Giles!'

'Yes, really my divinity. In a way you could say I've just shot my load – especially for you – *down under* the duvet!'

A tight lipped Sybil and an equally bewildered Francis sat in the First Class departure lounge waiting to board the Gulf Air flight for Abu Dhabi. A buoyant Jeremy along with Mark and even cheerful Tone were seated close by, a courtesy bottle of champagne on the table in front of them.

Meanwhile Tone continued repeating to himself his new mantra. Only a few more hours and then I'm going to make damn sure I find you, Tiffany love! Only a few more hours before I'm back on home ground!

'What the hell's happened?' muttered Sybil for the umpteenth time, 'or, more to the point, what *hasn't* happened?' In an aside to the long-suffering Francis he hissed, 'It's all a disaster! A total fuck up! What *could* have gone wrong?'

LONDON:

'Sybil, Giles. Something's screwed up! Seriously screwed up! Carpenter never came through in Sydney. I've had one of my contacts check out the various hotels and he eventually got lucky with the Park Hyatt. Our Mr Carpenter arrived there a week ahead of schedule but checked out after three days.'

'And?' Sybil's voice was tight.

'However, and herein lies the mystery, he was booked on the same flight as yours to Abu Dhabi but in tourist. My contact's now checking to see if he ever made the flight.'

'He's leaving it a bit tight, isn't he? Carpenter, I mean. It's now not one to go but still two to go!'

'He's obviously changed his mind…!'

'Obviously!'

'Obviously changed his mind and plans to carry out the dirty deed in Dhabi.'

'Let's hope so!' Sibyl's voice went up an octave. 'Do we know what this even Carpenter looks like?'

'According to Tiffany, a Neanderthal!'

'You mean typical Australian which means he won't be standing out in a crowd. Dhabi's crawling with them! At least an Englishman could look *English*!'

'Try and keep your hair on, dearest!'

'*Very* funny, Giles!'

'I am at times, aren't I my turtle dove of love?' Giles gave a light laugh. 'It may be a mere coincidence but Miss Tiffany is also behaving strangely – it's almost as if she's having second thoughts!'

'Well, it's too late for that! In for a penny, in for a pound!'

'And talking about pounds dear, some other rather disturbing news. Those payments made to our friend…'

'Don't tell me!'

''I have to, I'm afraid. When Julian hacked into his account – a practice run, he's under strict instructions not to do anything until Mr Carpenter has delivered – he discovered the wily bastard has already cashed all his funds to date.'

'But I thought it had been paid into an account in Switzerland?'

'They do have day return flights to Geneva, my darling.'

'Shit! How much has he had to date?'

'Half on account with the rest still to be paid on completion, plus that sweetener.'

'So there's still a further two hundred and fifty thou to go?'

'Exactly.'

'Well, I must say, I cannot see anyone throwing that sort of money away, unless…of my God, Giles. Blackmail!'

'I don't think Mr Carpenter would be that foolish, Sybs dear. He understands he's one alone and would never get away with it.'

'I hope you're right.'

'I *know* I'm right! Poor divinity. Oh! I've just managed to get myself hard again for you. Does Sybs want to play long distance wanks some more?'

'Oh Giles! I've just creamed my hands!'

'All the better to do the job with, my delicious, slimy Sybs!'

AUSTRALIA:

Nev, acting as next of kin, handed all details of Howie's unfortunate demise to the local police sergeant in the small, remote outback settlement near to where the fatal snake bite had taken place.

The sergeant proved to be a drunken, scrawny, broken-down wreck of a man who – as anticipated – had shown not even a flicker of interest in the incident. An equally drunken doctor, liberally sweating whisky from his pores following Nev's never-ending explanations, barely managed – again as anticipated – to sign the death certificate and the release forms.

'Thank you Alcoholics Not-At-All-Anonymous!' grinned Nev as he prepared to drive back to Sydney. 'He may be a bit ripe by the time I get him back,' Nev had informed the swaying, sweating doctor as he huddled over a new bottle of Grant's best, 'Pity I don't have a refrigerated truck!'

A vague, slurred suggestion by the doctor that he ask the barman for some extra ice was dismissed.

ABU DHABI:

'It's not going to happen!' Sybil, now semi-hysterical, shrieked into the telephone.

'Something must have happened,' said Giles soothingly, trying to keep his own agitation out of his voice.

Sybil finally lost his temper – a first ever for Giles. 'No Giles, he shouted. '*Nothing's* fucking happened, never was going to happen and never will! We've been conned, understand? Bloody c-o double n-e-d fucking conned!'

'Sybs!'

'Don't you fucking Sybs me! It's a disaster, a complete and utter disaster and someone, somewhere is going to pay for this!'

'Sybs! Sybil!' A distraught Giles beginning to panic at the sound of the old man's sobs coming over the phone. 'Sybs, *please!*' Now desperate he demanded, 'Is Francis there? Let me talk to him, please my darling!'

'Oh Giles, why? Why?' sobbed Sybil. 'It was all going to be so wonderful.'

'It still will be, my sweet, I promise. Now, let me speak to Francis, please. I insist'

'Giles!'

'Francis, get a doctor! Sybil obviously needs a sedative. In her present state God knows what she may do next! Do not, and I repeat, do *not* under any circumstances allow her near those three. *Under no circumstances*!'

'Yes, Giles,' whispered Giles. 'Oh *shit*!' he cried.

'What?'

'She's just rushed out of the door!'

'Stop her!'

'It's only the door to the balcony terrace!'

'*The balcony terrace*?' Giles's voice became a shriek. 'For God's sake she's probably going to jump!'

'Oh shit!' With a strangled cry Francis dropped the phone and dashed out onto the balcony only to find Sybil calmly surveying the distant desert scenery.

'Sybil!' he cried, 'you didn't!'

'Didn't what, precious?'

'Jump!'

'Jump? What on earth makes you think I'd jump? Surely you can't have you forgotten we've still got some serious unfinished shit to deal with?'

CHAPTER 13

'Why do I feel I'm part of an Enid Blyton children's adventure story, *The Famous Five Fuck Up*?' An angry Sybil sat glaring at Giles, Tiffany and Francis as the four sat around the dining table in Giles's flat. 'Franchot Seaton is now a household name – the Michel Bublé of the art world! – and here we are, a quarter of a million pounds plus down the drain and completely stymied! As for Jeremy...' Here Sybil's emotions overtook him and he responded by viciously spearing a piece of grilled soul with his fork.

'Mind the Meissen, dearest,' murmured Giles.

'*Fuck* the Meissen! If things had gone to plan we could have been buying the bloody Meissen factory by now!'

'Phone call, Mr Giles.' Martin, Giles's devoted, doddery old manservant, occasionally called Meth – short for Methuselah – in exasperation by his employer, stood apologetically in the doorway to the dining room.

'Didn't you tell the caller we were in the middle of dinner?' said Giles brusquely, almost to the point of rudeness.

'Of course I did, Mr Giles!' said the little man, his tiny frame bristling, 'But he said he simply *had* to talk to you!'

'Excuse me,' muttered Giles, crumpling up his table napkin and setting it next to his plate.

A gracious Sybil smiled at the old man still hovering in the doorway. 'He didn't mean it, Martin. Mr Giles has a lot on his mind at the moment.'

'At times…' muttered Martin. 'At times…'

'I know, I know,' soothed Sybil. 'But you can't teach an old dog new tricks!'

'But you can *whip* them!' announced Martin, causing the three to jump. 'You can always *whip* them!'

'That's quite enough, thank you Martin!' said Sybil sharply. 'We will ring when Mr Giles returns. Meanwhile, please ask Mrs Baring to hold back the soufflé until then.'

'Of course, Miss Sybil.' Bowing deferentially the old man turned and shuffled out with a distinct muttering of 'whip them!' trailing after him.

'What's this with the whipping?' asked Francis, giving a loud giggle, a mischievous glint in his eye.

'Didn't you know?' Tiffany gave a light laugh. 'Dear Meth, he's heavily into S and M though to look at him you'd never believe it in a trillion years!'

'And how do you know, dear?' This from Sybil.

'Oh, Meth and I are old mates. I arrived here slightly early one evening – Giles had been delayed at some function – and lo and behold Meth – I see you looking a bit puzzled Francis but that's Giles's nickname for him – became quite chatty. He spends his weekends in Tooting with a friend, a bus driver named Dez. Dez is also a part-time wrestler, known on the circuit as Danger Man Dez! When he's not punishing some poor bastard in the ring, Dez blissfully punishes Meth! It's a marriage made in bruises!'

'Bruised fruit!' chortled Francis.

'Or battered buggers!' giggled Sybil looking toward the door as Giles came back into the room.

'No wonder we've still got the gruesome twosome with us, Howie Carpenter's dead. From a snake bite for Christ's sake!'

'A snake bite? Tell me you're joking?' cried Sybil.

'I only wish I could,' said Giles sitting back down heavily. 'What a bloody bore,' he said looking at the three stunned faces.

'Who was that on the telephone?' This from a shocked Tiffany. Although Howie may have behaved badly he had, after all, been one terrific lover!

'And the body?' This from the more practical Sybil.

'It gets even more bizarre. From what my contact tells me – in answer to your question Tiffany that was Gus ringing from Australia – this colleague he was with made a wild attempt to drive the body back to Sydney or wherever but, after a day's driving, couldn't cope with our friend decaying by the minute and so *cremated him by the roadside!*'

'Now you are joking!' This from Tiffany.

'We *are* talking Australia, dear!' chimed in Sybil. 'It's a land where anything can happen' – and here he couldn't resist the dig – 'unless you *want* it to happen!'

'So, what now?' said Francis nervously, looking at the three.

'What now?' Tiffany gave a slow, almost beatific smile. 'We finish what we started but with one major twist.'

'And what may that be, my dear?' asked Giles, now intrigued by the young woman' cool demeanour.

'I get a bonus.'

'A bonus?' squawked Sybil. 'But we've already agreed how the money is to be– or would have been – divided.'

'I'm not talking about money Giles, I'm talking about something much more valuable.'

'Oh, for goodness sake, Tiffany! Spit it out!' snapped Sybil.

'Give me Franchot and I'll make sure you're rid of Jeremy and Mark!'

'What on earth are you talking about?' bellowed Giles. 'Franchot Seaton in *exchange* for Jeremy and Mark? Have you gone totally demented, my dear?'

'Yes, but demented in a very different way; I'm madly in love with the gorgeous Franchot Seaton and there's no doubt he's madly in love with me!'

Sybil, now regarding Tiffany with utter disbelief managed to splutter. 'In love with Franchot Seaton? And because of this *love* you want him spared while you *get rid of Jeremy and Mark*? Young woman, have you completely lost your mind?'

'Try me,' said Tiffany in a soft, calm voice. 'Have we got a deal?' She looked unflinchingly at Giles, then at Francis and finally back to Sybil. The old man's eyes flickered momentarily before he looked at Giles, giving a slight nod.

'Good,' said Tiffany. She gave the still stunned Sybil a bright, light smile. 'Perhaps now is a good time to give the all clear for that soufflé. All this talk of me becoming a murderess has suddenly made me feel quite hungry.'

'Is she for real?' asked Sybil.

Dinner over and Tiffany having left in a taxi, he, along with Giles and Francis were all sitting in Giles's private study.

'Let's wait and see,' said Giles placatingly as he poured him a large crème de menthe.

'I thought you'd say that,' smiled Sybil tiredly. 'But even with Jeremy and Mark out of the picture and obviously Franchot becoming part of the team, it does seem to me rather like shooting ourselves in the proverbial foot. I'm talking about blood money here.'

'But don't you see, my dear. After the demise of Jeremy, this terrible, terrible tragedy, our Phoenix – read that as Franchot! – rises from the ashes but, as you no doubt, my dear, used to so soothingly say, *Ashes to Ashes.* Mr Seaton is not infallible.'

'Plus he may not adhere to Miss Tiffany's charms!'

'Then we're fucked,' said Giles, resignedly.

'No Giles dear, not fucked. Totally fucked!'

'Franchot it's Tiffany.'

'I don't believe it! At last! My darling, darling lady, have I been trying to get hold of *you*! I told you I'd call you everyday and I *did*! But all I got was your voicemail.'

'Fifty seven.'

'Fifty seven?'

'The number of messages you left. I've kept them all!'

'You have? Oh Jeez!' Tone's delight was evident. 'Oh Tiffany, did you really keep them all?'

'All fifty seven! I was hoping you'd make it a round sixty but what's three missing messages between friends?'

'Are we friends, Tiffany?'

'I hope so Tone, may I call you Tone?'

'I thought you'd never ask! Your formal Franchot has always puzzled me. And, while you now will be calling me Tone may I, lovely Tiffany, call your lovely name at least a hundred times each day for the rest of my life?'

'Oh Tone!'

'Tiffany!'

'Where are you?'

'At this very minute? It may surprise you but I'm in a bookshop!'

'Bookshop?'

'Artists do read, you know! I'm in my favourite bookshop of all time, John Sandoe's in Chelsea, just off the Kings Road.'

'How desperate are you to see me?'

'Very!'

'Well, John Sandoe's is only a few minutes *run* from Cadogan Square!'

'I'm already in Draycott Place!'

'My, you are a fast worker, Mr Seaton! Will I have time to get my clothes off before you arrive?'

'If not, I'm not only a good runner, I'm also a good ripper!'

'As long as your middle name isn't Jack!'

Tone, now panting volubly, just managed to gasp, 'I'm just turning into Cadogan Gardens!'

'I'm ready and waiting!'

'Tone?' Tiffany, propped by against a mound of pillow, looked down at the handsome sleepy artist lying naked alongside her. 'You and Jeremy; how close *are* you?'

Tone raised a quizzical eyebrow. 'You mean, how close, close? Like being lovers?'

'Have you been lovers?'

Tone had the decency to look momentarily embarrassed. 'Well, er… yes, in a way… we have had sex together.'

'I have no doubts about that from what I can gather regarding jerk-off Jeremy! But, in your heart of hearts?'

'Heart of hearts, Tiffany?' Here Tone moved his huge torso up against the pillows, making himself more comfortable. 'I suppose I'm what people would call *bi* but my preference had always been for the ladies. Something amazing happened that evening seven days ago. For the first time in my life I fell deeply, hopelessly and gloriously in love!' Gently taking Tiffany's hand he added softly, 'Totally, completely and wholly in love.'

'Me too,' said Tiffany quietly. Brushing back her long dark hair, she in turn now took his large hand, gripping it tightly. Looking directly into his large brown smiling eyes, she added softly, 'Tone, you and Jeremy did a terrible thing together a few years ago, didn't you? A terrible, terrible thing.'

Tone's whole frame froze.

'What do you mean?' he croaked.

'And because of this terrible thing Jeremy now has a hideous hold over you and will do so for as long as he lives!'

''I don't know what you're talking about!' rasped Tone, beads of sweat appearing on his broad forehead.

'And everyday you look at Jeremy Spiers you know he *knows* and you are therefore ever captive in his thrall.'

'Stop it, Tiffany! Please stop it!' Tone's voice now reduced to a sob, he began to shake violently.

'Look at yourself, Tone.' Said Tiffany, her voice low and caressing. 'You're terrified Tone, aren't you? Terrified of bloody *Jeremy Spiers*!'

'Oh Christ! Oh Christ! Forgive me Tiffany! Oh Tiffany, what have I done?'

'What have you done? Why Tone you helped him kill my parents, that's what you've done, and now you're going to kill Jeremy and Mark for me!'

'It's done,' said Tiffany.

'What do you mean, *it's done*?' Giles held up a silencing finger at Sybil about to ask the same question.

'He'll do it. Get rid of Jeremy and Mark. Meet me in the Cadogan Hotel in half an hour and I'll explain all.'

Tiffany's revelation to Tone that the couple he'd helped Jeremy murder were, in fact, her parents saw a complete breakdown of the man, his only salvation being Tiffany's unawareness as to their torturous demise. Begging forgiveness he had lain sobbing in Tiffany's arms. After several minutes of soothing talk she finally whispered into his ear, 'Stop crying Tone, please stop crying. Make love to me instead. Why must you suffer when you are the innocent? Make love to me my beautiful Tone, Jeremy is the one who is evil, him and Mark!'

'Oh,' cried Tone as he slowly entered her forcing his thick, burgeoning cock deep into her moist, hot cunt. 'Oh my darling!' he gasped, 'can you ever forgive me?'

'With your enormous rod and your staff you comfort me!' whispered Tiffany before bursting into shrieks of laughter. 'Of course, I forgive you!' Her laughter contagious, Tone also began to laugh as he began to pound gloriously into her. 'That's it! That's right!' Tiffany began to gasp, 'Fuck me Tone, fuck me and forget! Harder, my love! Harder! From tonight and forever more it's only us to remember! *Harder*!'

Later, sitting on the toilet while an exhausted and finally pacified Tone slept, Tiffany calmly lit a cigarette, eyeing her fully seated image in the large mirror facing her.

'Do you really think you're in love with this guy?' she said to her reflection.

'Yes, why not?' her reflection answered.

'Even after what he did?'

'Even after what he was *told* to do!' corrected her reflection.

'Do you think this is forever?'

'Your mother was called Diamond,' said her reflection drily. 'Diamonds are meant to be for ever but she certainly wasn't!'

'So we take it day by day?'

'Day by day, Tiffany Cowper,' said her reflection. 'Now go and wake that ebony god and give him a mind-blowing blow job – maybe even have another fuck – then get him to take you out to dinner. Time to be seen on the scene and hey, Tiffany? Tone's sworn to secrecy as to who you are?'

'Absolutely!'

'So, off you go! Blow!'

When Tiffany was introduced to Jeremy as Mary Magdalene, his response was as expected, total disbelief. Barely able to keep a straight face – he had not recognised Tiffany, now a brunette and a striking young woman, as his childhood play mate – he managed a quick drink with the couple at The Botanist in Sloane Square before escaping to meet Mark back at the gallery.

'Let's hit the Wyndham!' he gasped. 'I need several of their really lethal Martinis!'

Minutes later, sitting overlooking the yacht marina Jeremy again burst into a fit of giggles. 'Forgive me, Marky. I saw a shadow moving near to one of the moored yachts over there and, for a magical moment, I could have sworn it was Tone *walking on water*!'

The two men's yelps of laughter reverberated across the placid scene and continued to do so for some time.

Three days later a red-eyed Jeremy called into the studio where a softly whistling Tone was working on a new canvas. Sybil, working nearby on another painting was, at the same time, in deep conversation with Francis working alongside him. As usual, he paid no attention to Jeremy's presence.

'Tone, can we talk? It's important!'

'I'm a bit busy at the moment, Jer. We do have an exhibition for Berlin to get ready, or have you and your *slave* driver lover forgotten your latest list of mind-boggling schedules for the workers?'

'It's Mark I want to talk about?'

'Oh oh! Trouble in the cosy love nest, is there?'

'He's disappeared!'

'What do you mean "disappeared?"' Tone said disinterestedly as he continued daubing some vibrant splashes of mauve onto his canvas.

'He hasn't been home for two days!'

'Two days?' Tone, feigning surprise, carried on painting. 'Is that unusual? Or maybe your loyal lover was out on a little illicit cruising and got lucky!'

'*Mark does not cruise!*' cried Jeremy vehemently. 'And I'm worried,' he added quietly.

'Maybe he's been abducted by an international gang for their hideous use and abuse in some gay *white* slave trafficking organisation!'

'This is not fucking funny, Tone! It's *serious*!' screamed Jeremy. 'I'm going to the police!'

'Be careful before you tread *that* path, Jer!' said Tone giving the distraught man a penetrating stare, 'Be very, very careful!'

'Go fuck yourself!' screeched Jeremy rushing out from the studio.

'What's upset our other lord and master?' said Sybil, peering at Tone from under his milk maid's cap, or 'inspirational headgear' as he preferred to call it. Tone's comment had been more down to earth. 'Rather like those things ladies wear when serving from behind the delicatessen counters in Tesco!' the big man had laughed.

'Mark's gone missing.'

'How lovely!'

'And Jeremy's upset!'

'Even more lovely!'

'And he wants to go to the police.'

'Not so lovely.'

'He won't, but we'll eventually have to report his disappearance ourselves and keep loose cannon Jeremy out of it. He's more than likely to throw a mega spanner into the works.'

Sybil gave a small sigh. 'We'd better call a meeting later and speak sensibly and calmly to the wretch.' He smiled at Tone, now definitely in favour. 'Who would have thought…'

'Who would have thought?' Tone gave a lewd laugh. 'Mark never forgot his one and only "Moan with Tone" and when I suggested a repeat performance the night before last, both he and his cock jumped at the opportunity!'

'So much for true love and his devotion to Jeremy! So, the dirty deed?'

'Where else but the original fuckery? All I'm prepared to say it was Nick the Nec all over again, well almost! Unless someone takes a look in one of those old freezing cabinets – just as well they were never removed! – I think you can safely say our problem is now well and truly put to rest!'

'I feel a distinct chill!'

'So, my dear Sybil, did Mark.'

That evening Giles, Sybil, Tiffany and Tone dined quietly at Eaton Square, Francis having left on the 16.04 Eurostar for Paris.

'Don't forget our lease is up in a few years time,' quipped Sybil as he daintily buttered a warm bread roll for Giles.

'By then, Sybil dear,' laughed Tone, 'Mark in the guise of a block of ice will have already gone with the flow! Geddit?'

'Good Old Father Thames!' laughed Tiffany.

CHAPTER 14

Mark's disappearance did not cause anything like the ruckus Jeremy had anticipated or secretly, hoped for, Mark being, after all, an associate of the now internationally recognised Spiers-Seaton Fine Arts phenomenon.

'Only a small mention in *The Times*,' he grumbled.

'Well, what did you expect, Jer?' said Tone, somewhat irritably, the two having met accidentally in the reception area of the gallery. 'He's only missing. It's not as if he's been murdered!'

'How do you know?' cried Jeremy.

'Well, I for one wouldn't even bother with murdering Mark, even though he was an obnoxious little prick!'

'There you are!' cried Jeremy, almost triumphantly. 'There you are! You said *was* as if he is dead instead of *is* as if he's only missing!'

'For fuck's sake, Jer, belt up!' Here Tone couldn't help adding, 'you've already got *two* murders under your *belt* so I shouldn't think, my friend, you'd want to associate yourself – however remotely – with a third! Therefore, if I were you, I'd stick to the missing theory!

'You bastard!' shrieked Jeremy. 'You two faced bastard!
Remember it took two pairs of hands to kill those Cowpers, yours
and mine!'

'Shut it, Jer!'

'What did you say?'

'I said shut it Jer. Not one word! Now you get the hell out of
here and into that office before I decide to punch in that pretty face
of yours! All of us, and I mean *all* of us have just had about enough
of you!'

'Oh really, well I've just about had enough of all of *you*!'

'Fine, well while you may think you've escaped a murder charge
I'll make bloody sure you get done for fraud!'

'Are you threatening me?'

'No, Jer, I'm telling you! After all it was *you* who instigated
the counterfeiting of my paintings and, as you are so fucking clever
at deceiving everyone, how on earth was I, being a simple artist and
black to boot, ever to know? Now get the fuck out of my sight!'

A seething Jeremy, muttering dire threats to all and sundry,
headed straight for the bar at the nearby Wyndham Grand Hotel.

'Your usual, Mr Spiers?' said the smiling barman.

'Please, but make it a triple!'

Fucking black cunt, seethed Jeremy, glaring out over the marina,
sparkling in the lunchtime sunshine. Fucking ignoramus! Who turned
you into fucking Franchot Seaton, an art legend in his own time? Me,
you piece of black shit! Me, Jeremy Spiers! Gesturing for a second
Martini, tears forming, he sat gazing out at the blurred scene in front
of him.

'Oh Marky,' he said in a soft, tearful, almost self-pitying
whisper, 'Where the fuck are you or, even worse, what the fuck has
happened to you?' Taking another sip of his second drink his mind
veered back to the sneering Tone. 'Uppity shit!' he suddenly spat out,
much to the astonishment of a pair of middle-aged matrons enjoying
a quiet glass of wine. 'Sorry ladies.' He smiled apologetically, 'Girl
friend problems.'

'Oh,' murmured the one obviously thinking, No wonder you've got problems with your girl friend, young man, if you refer to her as an uppity shit!

It was late afternoon by the time Jeremy stumbled from the hotel, blinking at the unexpected brightness outside – he had moved from the bar terrace back into the cooler atmosphere of the bar itself after feeling the alcohol beginning to take its toll. Fuck, he thought, I can't go back to the gallery like this. Alexis (the receptionist) can cope. What I really need is a bit of release from all this and that's release with a capital R.

Following the attack on the Cowpers, Jeremy had done his best to keep his psychopathic tendencies under control. The embryonic period involving the setting up of the gallery plus its growing success had done much to keep his innermost demons at bay. His stabilising relationship with Mark had also been a major factor in his keeping a calmer countenance. However, fuelled by alcohol and a terrifying foreboding, the demons in his brain once again took over. Gesturing to the doorman to get him a taxi, Jeremy managed to clamber into the back without thinking clearly.

'Where to, guv?' asked the driver glancing in his rear view mirror at the obviously very drunk young man.

'Anywhere, but fucking here,' slurred Jeremy, collapsing against the back seat.

'Anywhere but fucking here,' mumbled the taxi driver. 'Fucking great!' Giving another glance at his passenger now sitting with his eyes closed, the driver made his mind up. Fucking pouf! he thought. Take him up to the West End and leave him somewhere in that Old Compton Street. Rich looking sod like him will either pick up, get picked up, get his dick sucked, get fucked or get his bloody head bashed in! Who gives a fuck as long as he pays the fare!

'You've stopped,' slurred Jeremy, 'Where are we?'

'Old Compton Street,' said the driver.

'Why?' questioned Jeremy querulously.

'You said anywhere so I brought you here,' came the curt reply.

'Oh, how kind of you!' said Jeremy, sneeringly, 'How very fucking kind of you!'

'Oi! Out of my fucking cab now! And you owe me twenty quid!'

'Your need is obviously greater than mine, *cabbie*!' said Jeremy patronisingly throwing a twenty pound note through the driver's window, the note hitting the startled man in the face.

By this time Jeremy had managed to get himself out of the taxi and was standing swaying in the street.

'You're a tenner short!' (he was not) snarled the driver, now red-faced with fury and about to get out of the cab and give the arrogant young man a severe trouncing.

'Oh, I do so beg your pardon!' said Jeremy with all the sarcasm he could muster. Peeling off another twenty pound note he dropped this through the window onto the driver's lap. 'Big bollocks,' he said, looking in and glancing down at the man's bulging flannels. 'Big cock too it seems. You wouldn't fancy a blow job, would you?'

'Fuck you, pouf!' bellowed the driver before roaring off with a squeal of tyres.

'Up yours, arsehole!' sniggered Jeremy looking vaguely at the doorway to the pub where he'd been dropped.

'Sounds fun!' said a camp voice.

'What?' Jeremy turned his reeling head slowly in the direction of the voice.

'Sounds fun,' said the voice again, a little louder this time.

'Where are you? slurred Jeremy.

'Peek-a-boo! Right behind you!'

'What the fuck!' Jeremy slowly turned around to find himself facing a well built, chunky young man whom, apart from the voice, looked more Tom Cruise than Tomasina.

Jeremy's hidden forces went into overdrive. 'Well, peek-a-boo to you too! Whoever you are!' He squinted at the smiling young man. 'A bit camp for a pick up line if I may say so? You *are* trying to pick me up, I take it?'

'I don't know yet,' said Tom/Tomasina in his strange falsetto. 'Maybe after you've bought me a drink or two I'll let you know.'

Jeremy pointed to the doorway of Comptons pub. 'After you,' he said gallantly, attempting a small bow which ended in a stumble saved by the door jamb.

Once inside the dim interior Jeremy found his head clearing and his sense of dizziness disappearing. Getting his bearings he looked again at the still smiling young man. 'You order, I'm buying. I'll have a vodka on the rocks, a double, double vodka on the rocks!'

'One double, double coming up!'

'I'm Jeremy, by the way,' said Jeremy reaching for his wallet and taking out another twenty pound note.

'I'm Tom.'

You've *got* to be joking! Jeremy thought. 'Hi Tom!' he said.

Having settled themselves in one of the darker corners of the pub, Jeremy sat studying the young man intently, his mind whirring. Such a long time since I had any real Jeremy-type fun, he said to himself, such a long, long time so why not treat yourself to some of that almost forgotten fun today? Mark's obviously buggered off for a day or two – the tears and fears of Mark's disappearance overcome by the pheromones now passing between him and this Tom – more than likely with that Bryan Wilder he's never stopped talking about (Bryan being another artist exhibiting at the gallery). His head beginning to throb with a too long denied excitement, he asked, 'Where do you live, Tom?'

'I have a small houseboat near Chelsea Bridge.'

'Christ,' said Jeremy, 'Talk about coincidence! I've just come from over there.'

'Oh, you live in the same area then?'

'No,' said Jeremy, always wily but now being extra cautious. 'I'm just visiting London for a few days. I'm staying at the Wyndham over at Chelsea Harbour.'

'And where do you live when you're not staying at the Wyndham,' asked Tom innocently, thinking, You fucking wanker, you're that Jeremy Spiers and you have that quite famous gallery off Lots Road. I've seen you in endless magazines and papers and I've also seen you driving around with that poncey black artist in his BMW sports!

'Paris,' said Jeremy for want of somewhere to say. 'I have an apartment on the Avenue Foch!'

'*Naturellement*!' said Tom.

'What do you want from me?' Jeremy suddenly demanded, his blood lust and temper beginning to take over. 'You obviously want something otherwise we wouldn't be sitting here!'

'Whoa! Down boy, down! Sure I fancy you,' said Tom, 'but keep your knickers on!'

'The only point in fancying anyone,' snarled Jeremy, 'is to get their fucking knickers *off*!'

'OK, you win!' said Tom, letting out a camp, high pitched nervous laugh. (Christ, thought Jeremy, you're perfect for what I want, need. Hopefully that fucking choir boy's voice doesn't mean you haven't a set of balls to go with your looks!).

Tom gave the strangely behaving young man another quick glance, thinking, No, he must be OK. Christ he's a public figure and all that plus he also has that boyfriend so it must be alright. He pointed at their nearly empty glasses. 'Let's finish theses and head back to my place.' He gave a light laugh. 'I don't suppose it would look quite right you taking someone up to your room dressed like this?'

'Suite,' said Jeremy, thinking, You're bloody fucking right, my friend, dressed in those sprayed on jeans and a T shirt saying 'Blow Jobs Are Better Than No Jobs.'

'Sorry, suite,' said Tom with a grin at his play on the word. 'And of course you couldn't allow yourself to be seen dead with someone dressed like this.'

Don't be so sure, thought Jeremy, a rush of adrenalin suddenly coursing thought his veins. 'Let's get a cab,' he said instead.

Hailing a passing taxi they both clambered into the back, Tom issuing directions in his high pitched voice.

Christ, thought Jeremy panicking. What if he's a dyke? One of those diesel types but with a pure feminine voice. Shit! Just my fucking luck! 'Tom,' he said, as the taxi wended its way around a congested Trafalgar Square, 'you *are* a bloke?'

'Why, do you think I'm not?' laughed the young man, not at all thrown.

'No, but er...'

'My voice? It's the pits, isn't it? The big let down! Pity I can't sing otherwise I would have made a great castrato!' Tom gave another light laugh. 'No, the meat and two veg is certainly there! Quite impressive as you'll soon be finding out!'

'What about a preview?'

Tom pointed ahead to the dull box shape of Buckingham Palace looming up ahead as they proceeded along The Mall. '*Not* in front of her Maj!' he said camply. 'It's tough enough being the real Queen without having rivals flashing their own orbs and sceptres as they drive past!'

It was dark as the driver dropped them off by the line of houseboats, a picturesque floating village moored on the Thames near to Chelsea Bridge. 'Mine's the last one at the end,' informed Tom as they proceeded gingerly along the wooden walkway linking the boats. 'Most are closed up at this time of year so we can yell our hearts out and nobody will hear – or to put it another way – who gives a fuck if they did?'

'I forgot to ask, what do you do for a living,' said Jeremy, clinging to the swaying handrail. 'Shit!' he exclaimed, nearly losing his footing. 'I'm not sure whether I'm still pissed or it's the fucking walkway that's swaying!'

'Both,' laughed Tom. 'I'm a chef, by the way and were here, *Roam Sweet Roam*!'

'What?'

'Instead of *Home Sweet Home* as she's a boat I decided on *Roam Sweet Roam*!'

'Well, I suppose it's slighter better than *Foam Sweet* fucking *Foam*!' muttered Jeremy.

At Jeremy's insistence Tom had bought a bottle of vodka along with two bottles of wine from over the bar counter. 'Christ, we can stop at an Off Licence, Jeremy,' he had complained at Jeremy's insistence they purchase a few bottles from the pub to take with them. 'The prices in here will be extortionate!'

'Why complain if you're not paying?' had been Jeremy's grandiose reply.

'You actually *live* here?' said Jeremy looking at the small but cosy quarters with disdain.

'I know it's not the Ritz,' said Tom defensively, 'but its mine and its home!'

'You mean *roam,* came the spiteful reply.

'I'll get the glasses,' muttered Tom who by now having second thoughts about taking things any further with the strange young man. Turning to Jeremy, about to ask him what mix he'd like with his vodka, he was caught by a heavy blow on the side of his head knocking him unconscious.

'Oh, you've got a pair of balls alright, a very pretty, most impressive pair. Pity they seem to have malfunctioned in making you sound like a man!' came the distant voice. 'Nice cock too, massive in fact and uncut which is certainly going to add to the fun. What are you? Seven inches? Yes, it must be at least seven! Goodness, we *are* going to have some fun and games this evening!' The voice took on a weird, quivering, castrato-like falsetto. 'We can scream to our heart's content, can we? Nobody can hear us and who gives a fuck if they did? Oh, goody, goody, *goodness*! Yes, we are certainly going to have some fun!'

A gradually awakening Tom, to his horror, found himself gagged and unable to make any distinctive sounds. Furthermore he had been stripped naked and bound securely to a small upright kitchen chair with twine, his hands tied crushingly behind his back. Feeling a searing pain in his groin he stared wildly down only to see his balls purple and distended to the point of bursting, tightly bound at the top by another piece of twine. His horror grew tenfold when he summoned up the courage to look at his throbbing cock. Tied to the end of his foreskin was heavy glass jug – the one used for his daily morning juice – a piece of twine threaded though the handle, the jug semi-filled with what could only have been Jeremy's piss. Tom's foreskin had been stretched until only a thin, veined, pink transparent ribbon of an additional five inches.

Tom, his eyes rolling in panic, began threshing his head wildly, 'Mm! Mm! Mm' his attempted screams completely muffled.

Jeremy pointed to the small gas hob where a saucepan of water was staring to boil and to a kettle on the adjoining hob, with steam spurting violently from its spout.

'I once boiled my sister Emmie's little fishies once,' announced Jeremy in an eerie sing-song voice, 'but I've never boiled anyone's balls before!'

Tom, eyes bulging, began to shudder violently.

'But first we must dock Boris's tail!' The sing-song voice was now spookily child-like. 'After all, he's not a Labrador so nasty, nasty tail must go!'

Taking a serrated edged bread knife from where he had set this along with some other kitchen appliances, Jeremy began to saw through Tom's over-stretched foreskin, blood spurting violently out over the spasmodic young man's bound feet.

'Now the fishies!' crooned Jeremy, 'Emmie's naughty, naughty' – and here his voice dropped back to its normal tenor – 'boring, fucking fishies!'

Lifting the saucepan of boiling water from the hob he positioned it under Tom's distended balls before raising it up and immersing them in the still bubbling liquid.

Even through the gag Tom's screams were audible; screams of pure pain and undiluted terror.

'Clever, clever Jeremy,' said the falsetto child-like voice again. 'Ballsy wallsys fit the saucepan perfectly! Clever, clever Jer!'

He looked at Tom who, having passed out, was slumped forward on the chair. 'Oh, how *dull!*' said Jeremy crossly. Removing the saucepan from the young man's now boiled and even more bloated balls he picked up a metal meat skewer. 'Well Tom,' he said looking at the silent figure, 'you did say you were a chef and my, oh my, even at dear little *Roam Sweet Roam* you do have a fascinating array of cooking toys!'

Checking out the gleaming pointed tip in the soft lamplight from the bulkhead, Jeremy's face broke into a grin as, beginning a squeaky rendition of *Pop Goes The Weasel,* he repeatedly jabbed the skewer into Tom's bloated, boiled balls.

'Oh, gooey, gooey glug, glug!' he gurgled as he got down onto his knees, eagerly licking the red and opaque sebaceous liquid oozing from the wounds.

'Dinner! Ah yes, dinner! Dinner can't be served until we've had a bit more fun!' With surprising deftness Jeremy hacked off Tom's cock and remaining foreskin before picking up the other piece still attached to the jug lying on the floor. Placing these on a small chopping block he then diced them neatly with a meat cleaver found in one of the kitchen drawers.

Untying the silent, mutilated body he gently carried Tom over to the neat bunk bed, laying him face downwards over the edge. Jeremy, himself also naked during the whole scenario, stood idly playing with his still rampant erection as he stood looking at the pale white back below him.

'*Blemishes*! Jeremey wants to play blemishes!' he announced to the silent cabin. Having remembered seeing a packet of cigarettes in the back pocket of Tom's jeans, he now reached for one from the discarded pair, taking a cigarette out of the packet. Lighting this from the still burning gas ring he took a deep draw creating a bright, red glowing tip.

'*Blemishes*!' he crooned. '*Blemi time*!' he crooned again as he began to dot out *Roam Sweet Roam* in sizzling burns on Tom's pristine back.

'Who the fuck ever heard of a fucking *Roam Sweet Roam*?' he growled, his voice back to normal. 'Fuck *Roam Sweet* fucking *Roam*' he snarled and promptly did just that.

Half an hour later, after a light meal prepared from a packet of pasta found in a cupboard along with a jar of pasta mix into which Tom's diced foreskin and cock had been simmered, a satiated Jeremy – having greedily eaten the mixture and announced to the silent cabin 'that was fucking delicious!' – sat calmly in the chair formerly occupied by Tom, finishing off the bottle of Merlot bought earlier. 'Now Tom,' he said to the silent form – he had been forced to knock Tom out again after the young man had started coming to and, now without his gag, begun screaming in pain and terror – 'as you will soon see, when you least expect it, you get it! Now we're about to play Vikings!'

Reaching for his wrist watch which had been left on the draining board, he checked the time. 'Ah, the witching hour is almost upon us and for you, castrato Tom, a twitching one as well! I did say we were about to play Vikings, didn't I? So, let's play! A body, even when unconscious, still twitches and turns when it burns. Its acrobatics can be quite breathtaking. Pity I won't be here to witness it all!'

Cleaning himself thoroughly before putting on his clothes, Jeremy then took a dishtowel from near the sink, laying it on the still burning gas ring. Next, throwing the unconscious Tom onto the small, cramped floor space, he pulled off the coverlet from the bunk bed, adding one end of this to the brightly burning dishtowel. 'This will soon be a case of *Foam Sweet Foam* after all when the fucking fire brigade gets here,' cackled Jeremy as the flames began to take hold. 'Talk about fucking irony!' Clambering out from the burning houseboat – the glow of the flames readily visible through the small porthole windows – Jeremy made his way quickly and silently back to the gallery.

Having reached the sanctuary of the building – he could hear the distant sound of the fire engines on their way to the scene – Jeremy did as his usual wont, simply called and arranged a cab with the company's regular taxi service, secure in the knowledge it would be seen as a routine booking. It was not unusual for either him, Tone Sybil or Francis to use the taxi service at odd hours both day and night.

The unfortunate burning of the three houseboats made little impact, their importance usurped by a bomb scare in the West End. Tom's charred remains plus evidence of a broken vodka bottle and two wine bottles had simply been put down to an unfortunate drunken accident. As one of the other houseboat owners was heard to say, 'It could have been worse. Fortunately for the owners of the other two boats they are still away. Bet they won't be too pleased on their return! The young man who died? No, know nothing about him. A chef I hear. Well, he certainly burned the bloody dinner then, didn't he?'

CHAPTER 15

'It's him! I know it's him! He's managed to keep himself under control but Mark's disappearance has triggered off the whole shebang again!'

'Shebang?'

'Matter – hidden feelings, whatever!'

'How can you be so sure?' An anxious Tiffany looked at Tone, the two of them sitting side by side in a taxi on their way to a launch party for bestselling author Robin Anderson's latest book.

'It's got all the trappings,' said Tone. 'Young Tom Billings, whose boathouse was burned along with him in it? He was gay.'

'So?'

'So? It's too much of a coincidence.' Tone looked back at Tiffany. 'Out of interest, I checked with our cab booking service; Jeremy booked a cab from the gallery back to his flat soon after midnight, the night of the fire.'

'But that doesn't incriminate him?'

'Christ, Tiffs, it's the evening of the afternoon he told me Mark was missing! Instead of sympathising with him or giving him any support, I simply made fun of the situation. It was at the same time that I warned him about going to the police.'

'But he could have been at the gallery for some other reason? He does spend some rather strange hours there – they both did!'

'Do, Tiffs, do! Mark's not officially dead remember!' Tone was silent for a moment as the cab made its way along towards the venue. 'Originally, when we were just starting off we'd all be in and out of the place at all hours. Now we're more established and all seem – or seemed – to have gotten our personal lives sorted out' – here he gave a small smile and squeezed Tiffany's hand – 'the gallery's usually deserted after eight at the latest, unless we have a function going on.'

'So where could he have gone to have met up with this Tom?'

''According to our friendly barman at the Wyndham – a jokey comment made in passing, nothing derogatory – Jer became very, very pissed that particular afternoon and suddenly left without even bothering to sign the bill, something he never, ever forgets, hence the barman remembering. He must have got straight into a cab out front of the hotel and fucked off somewhere.'

'With something in mind?'

'With something very unpleasant in mind! Jeremy is now someone to be very concerned about, very. Both you and I know what he's capable of when driven to it.'

'Have you spoken to Sybil?'

'Not as yet, but I think we all ought to meet a.s.a.p!' He glanced at his watch. 'How long do you think we'll be at this bash?'

'Oh, just long enough to say hello to Robin and buy his book. Now there's another one. Looking at Robin you'd never think such a lurid, sordid mind could be lurking behind that charming persona! Rather like Giles's Meth and his S and M! You never know what goes on behind those benign faces!'

'I'm calling Giles now. Perhaps we can meet later this evening.' Tone was about to reach for his mobile when it rang. Looking at the caller's identification Tone gave Tiffany a quick glance. 'Speak of the devil! Yes Giles?'

Tiffany was able to hear Giles's plummy voice coming over the static. 'Franchot, are you with Tiffany? Good! We have to talk. It sounds as if you're in a taxi so you're obviously en route to some sordid bacchanal! Can you meet self and Sybs later? Say ten at Eaton Square?' On hearing Tone's quiet affirmative, Giles clicked off.

'I think it's time,' said Tone, clutching Tiffany's hand again.

'I'm with you, my darling, all the way!'

'Marry me, Tiffs!' said Tone as their cab drew up outside their destination.

'We're engaged!

'You're *what*?'

'Engaged. Tone and me!'

'Well…' a shaken Sybil looked at the smiling couple. 'Well, congratulations,' he just managed to say.

'A bit sudden isn't it?' said Giles jocularly.

'Not when you know its right!' said Tone firmly but along with a broad grin. He looked at Giles, 'Nothing fancy, a registry office "do" and I'd like you to be my best man, Giles, if that's OK with you?'

'And you, Sybil, the other witness,' smiled Tiffany.

'I couldn't think of anything nicer,' came the clipped reply.

'This calls for a bottle of champagne! Excuse me for a moment while I sort out Meth.'

'I'll come with you, dear' said Sybil, taking Giles by the arm. 'We'll leave you two lovebirds to bill and coo!'

In the hallway Sybil turned to Giles, 'What the *hell* is the girl up to? She asked up to spare Franchot – which we've done –but marrying him? I see nothing but complications ahead.'

'Likewise.'

'My God, Giles! Don't you see? If she marries Franchot, Tone or whatever, and something untoward does happen to him, she more than likely ends up with all his works!'

'And more! How many Seatons do you really know of apart from those in the gallery plus the ones you and Francis have been working on? For all we know Franchot may very well have another flat – God forbid *another studio* – where he has a selection stored while secretly painting more. After all, his time is his own.'

'Talk about turnabout!'

'And of course with damn Jeremy now a very loose keg who simply has to be dealt with meaning' – raising their eyebrows rose they both said in unison – 'Spiers-Seaton Fine Arts basically becomes Franchot's!'

'And in the event of something still happening to Franchot, Tiffany Seaton to-be ends up owning two thirds of the business!' This from Giles.

'Over my dead body!' glowered Sybil.

'Don't tempt fate, dear! Now I think we'd better organise that champagne, hadn't we?'

''Got any arsenic whilst we're about it?' said Sybil drily.

Tone and Tiffany decided to keep their engagement secret, one of the main reason's being Tiffany's true identity being exposed.

'God knows his reaction when he does find out,' said Tiffany.'

'He'll go ape shit!' said Tony without any rancour. He smiled adoringly at the young woman. 'The sooner you become Mrs Tiffany Seaton, the better.'

'For the moment it will have to be Mary Seaton, Tone and don't you dare forget it! Again, don't – not even for a second – dare forget you still have to deal with jerk-off bloody Jeremy!'

'I've been thinking about that…' Tone began.

'Don't you – not for a split second – even *begin* thinking about reneging on our deal!' snapped Tiffany, eyes blazing. 'I may be in love with Franchot Seaton but I don't wish to spend the rest of my life with a coward!'

'Christ Tiff! That's a bit low.'

'Oh Tone, let me assure you, I can go much lower than that! Put it this way, any further talk of marriage is on hold until Spiers is well and truly out of the way, i.e. dead.'

'Christ, Tiffs…'

'Not Christ, Tone. Jeremy.' Tiffany sat looking defiant. 'I'll give you two weeks Tone and then, if Mr Spiers is still around polluting out lovely planet, I'm calling the whole thing off.'

'You can't be serious?' said Tone imploringly.

'I can be very serious, Tone, so don't go there.'

''You wouldn't?' said Tone, his handsome face sagging with disbelief.

'Don't push it Tone! Remember, I could suddenly miss Mummy and Daddy very much; so much so I begin to air my suspicions about their unfortunate demise.'

'You bitch!'

'No Tone, just warning you just how unpleasant and how spectacular your fall from grace could be. So, two weeks.'

'No, Tiffany, I'll do it in my own time and when I'm ready. For all his misgivings, Jeremy and I go back a long way and there is still a strong bond.'

'Yes I'm sure, being the murderers involved in a double crime must be quite – as you put it – bonding. Or should that be binding?' Tiffany picked up her handbag. 'Now are we lunching or not? I could simply *die* for some of *Scalini's* lobster pasta!'

Tones' consternation at Tiffany's prevaricating saw them sitting mostly in silence throughout lunch, their conversation stilted. Only the apologetic interruptions by several admirers coming over to Tone to congratulate him on his work broke the ever growing tension.

'Isn't that Francis and Jean Claude who've just come in?' said Tone, the relief in his voice apparent. It was only afterward, following the ensuing fracas, he realised though he had mentioned them to her, Tiffany had never met the two.

'This is all we need,' muttered Tiffany, 'The famous Mademoiselle Francois and her French Connection!'

'Don't, Tiff. They're friends, and Francis – like Sybil – is indispensable.'

'Tone!' Francis's surprise at seeing the artist sitting with a glamorous stranger was obvious.

'Francis! Jean Claude!' Without looking at Tiffany, Tone hurriedly continued. 'Why don't you join us for a quick drink before you lunch? We're about to have our coffee and grappas. Please.' Beckoning a nearby waiter to bring over two more chairs he turned to a smirking Tiffany, saying with an eager-to-please demeanour, 'Mary, you've heard me speak of the famous Francis? Well, this is he! And this charming French import is Jean Claude, a friend from Paris.'

'Mary Magdalene,' said Tiffany with a brittle smile. 'Blessed, I'm sure!'

'Likewise Mademoiselle Mary …' said Jean Claude, a puzzled expression marring his handsome face.

'Oh please, simply call me Mary. We don't stand for religious ceremony these days!'

'Er …Mary,' said Jean Claude looking even more confused.

'I'm Francis,' said Francis, smiling pleasantly.

'Is that with an *e* or and *i*?' smiled Tiffany, her smile more tight than ever. 'I'm told there is a difference. Something to do with gender I believe.'

'Please sit,' said Tone, pointing desperately at the two vacant chairs.

'I think we'll go straight to our table,' said Francis primly. 'And it's with an *i,* Miss Magdalene,' he added sibilantly, taking a startled Jean Claude firmly by the arm.

'That was both rude and unfair,' snapped Tone as the couple moved away.

'Unfair? You're the one who refers to him as Paint Francis of The Sissy! Not me! I suppose that's the stud?'

'Jean Claude's his lover, not his stud.

'Whatever. Lucky little Francis with an *i.'*

'What's got into you, Tiffs? I've never heard you be so uncharitable!'

'Two things, Tone dear. One, you got into me – several times – earlier today, which is always delicious and two; you're developing cold feet, which isn't!'

'I told you I'd deal with it!'

'Seeing is believing.'

'Please don't start.'

'You haven't seen anything yet!'

'I'd better get the bill.'

'Better still, why not go and join the love birds? Who knows, you may even get lucky. A *ménage á trios* perhaps?' Picking up her handbag and without a backward glance Tiffany stalked out of the busy restaurant.

'May I join you?'

'But of course, Tone. Mary Magdalene had to suddenly leave, did she?' asked Francis sarcastically. 'A blessing to attend, perhaps.'

'A hair appointment,' muttered Tone, not rising to the bait.

'Well, she certainly doesn't need a manicure, does she?' snapped Francis. 'Her talons are sharp enough!'

'I'm sorry about all that,' mumbled Tone, deeply uncomfortable. 'Put it down to nerves... er...we've just become engaged.'

'You can't be serious?' squeaked Francis.

'Deadly,' said Tone drily.

Francis gave the big man a long look. 'You're mad,' he said simply. 'Totally mad. That young woman's a fucking ticking bomb!'

'Shut it, Francis,' said Tone warningly. 'That's the girl I'm going to marry!'

'No, *you* shut it Tone!' cried Francis, his voice rising shrilly, so much so that several diners turned towards where the strange trio were sitting. 'We came out for a quiet lunch together. We didn't expect to see you and we certainly didn't expect you to gate crash our table! Now, if you don't mind, please fuck off and Tone, for your information – I've already told Sybil – should I decide to continue with reproducing any more of your so-called paintings, thus assisting you in this ridiculous farce of your so-called phenomenal output, these will be counterfeited, copied whatever, in Paris. I'm moving to Paris, for good, this coming weekend.'

'But you can't!' Tone's harsh voice echoed eerily through the now silent – and riveted – restaurant.

'But I can and I am, Tone! So, instead of sitting there like a complete moron please do as I suggested a few minutes ago. Kindly fuck off!'

Tone silently got to his get, his face wracked with humiliation. Ignoring the silent diners he made his way steadily towards the exit, but not before escaping Francis's camp voice cutting clearly through the hush, 'Maybe Franchot Seaton is going back to his studio to actually *paint* one of his own paintings!'

The thoroughly mortified man stood outside the restaurant, visibly sweating, his head pounding. Making his way slowly along picturesque Walton Street, his head clearing by the minute, he made his decision. Reaching for his mobile, he punched in a number. 'Jer,' he said with no preamble, 'Like fucking Houston we've got a mega problem. I know you're hurting and I'm sorry.' Tone gave a deep gulp. 'We have to talk. Redcliffe in about twenty minutes? You're on.'

CHAPTER 16

'She's *who*?'

'Mary Magdalene is Tiffany Cowper. She's asked me to kill you.'

Jeremy sat staring at Tone, his mouth slack. 'Tell me this is a sick, sick joke,' he slurred.

'No joke, Jer, no joke at all. They're all in on it, Sybil, Giles Delaware and Tiffany Cowper. Tiffany wants me to kill you in revenge for her parents' death and, the more I think about it, I'm next on the list after you!' Tone calmly took a sip of his wine. 'It all makes sense. Yes. I fell for Tiffany but not for the Tiffany now revealing her true self. Whether it was through sheer coincidence we met, I'll never know but it all seems to fit.'

'Christ, talk about swings and roundabout!' Jeremy gave a hollow laugh, reaching for the wine bottle. 'You must admit Tone, it *is* the biggest sick joke of the century! What you're really saying is Tiffany Cowper "suddenly" – in inverted commas, no make that perverted! – appears on the scene wanting both you and me done away and then, hey presto! It's Giles, Sybil Tiffany – the latter having hooked *you* – and you lot wanting *me* dead! Fucking hell…'

What Jeremy didn't say was he and Mark had been planning to get rid of Tone and Sybil along with Francis.

What Tone didn't say was he'd already killed Mark.

'We're really back to square one, aren't we Tone?'

'Square one, Jer. Tiffany Cowper now has this diabolical hold over us – she knows we killed her folks – as do Giles and Sybil.'

'So, what now?' The two looked steadily at each other.

'You killed that boy the other night, didn't you, Jer?' said Tone softly.

'Just like you killed Mark, Tone.'

Tone gave a great start, spilling most his wine over his Armani trousers. 'What are you talking about?' he stammered.

'Oh, come on, Tone! Refrigerators tend to make a noise when in use, albeit a slight one. Why, all of a sudden, should the freezer cabinets in Nev's fuckery suddenly have sprung to life? I mean, they've been out of action all the time we've been here!'

Tone remained sitting in a shocked silence, the wine dribbling unimpeded down his trouser legs.

'Cabinet number six, Tone. I checked them all.'

'Jer, I don't know…'

'Don't even think about it, Tone. Simply regard it as another bizarre twist in a twisted chain of events! My initial shock and anger was replaced by a strange curiosity so I did it, the other night!'

'Did what?'

'I turned off the refrigerator system in the morning, giving Mark time to thaw out a bit and then fucked him in the afternoon. Strange, very strange but also tingly exhilarating!'

'Jesus, Jer!'

'He won't last for much longer what with being continually frozen and then defrosted. He's actually beginning to feel a bit mushy. He's switched off again for a final session this evening.' Jeremy casually lit a cigarette. 'I wouldn't say no to some help and, as you *did* kill him, I think it's fair you *do* help me.'

'Jesus!'

'And talking about Jesus, that brings us back to Tiffany, Mary fucking Magdalene Cowper!'

'Shit yes!'

'Let me get us something stronger. I think Spiers-Seaton have a great deal of planning to do.'

Returning with a filled ice bucket, an unopened bottle of Stolichnaya and two glasses, Jeremy filled these to the brim before continuing. Sitting comfortably he gave a small laugh. 'So, as I've said, Spiers-Seaton again, is it?'

'It is!'

'Great. Let's face it Tone, with my inheritance plus the shitloads of money we've been pulling in, we're rich enough to sit back for a bit and watch the sunset, should we so wish.' He reached for a small note pad and pen lying on the coffee table. Writing as he spoke he listed the names. 'We now have Giles, Sybil, Francis and Tiffany all as potential powder kegs and all, in their own way, highly inflammable fuses.'

'Right.'

Jeremy tapped the pad thoughtfully. 'Could this Jean Claude be a problem? How much does he know?'

'Not a lot. In fact, I think we can take it he's a hundred per cent ignorant. He may have set up the place in Paris and only sees Francis and an artist – and obviously a fabulous fuck – but nothing more! He's more of a glorified part-time gofer for Giles. He also helps in the family stationary business in Paris.'

'I'll put him down anyway, along with a question mark. Giles may not have been as discreet with him as we may think he has.'

Jeremy looked across at Tone. 'Are you alright with this, Tone? I mean, a few days ago this Tiffany Cowper was the most important happening in your whole life.'

'Was Jer, was!'

'She showed me her cunt once, you know!' Jeremy gave a light laugh.

'She *what*?' Tone let out an incredulous laugh. 'Tell me you're joking!'

'I'll do more than tell you I'm joking. I'll tell you the story!'

An hour later a fully impaled, bucking, twisting and panting Tone violently rode a whimpering, gasping Jeremy.

'Oh Tone, oh Tone!' Jeremy groaned followed by a sobbing, 'So good, so bloody fucking good!'

'As they say,' grunted Tone rapidly approaching his climax, 'Once you've been with a black you'll never go back! Ah *shit*! I'm coming, Jer! I'm fucking coming! Ahhhhh!'

Lying comfortably side by side, their hands gently clasped together, Jeremy suddenly let out a small, camp giggle.

'What?' asked a smiling Tone.

'Our pact to sort this out!'

'Yeah?'

'Well, ordinarily a pact such as ours is usually sealed in blood.'

'So?'

'We've just sealed it in semen!'

Three days later David Spiers was fatally injured in a hit and run accident in the King's Road. The culprit was never to be found.

'One down, three or maybe four to go,' said Tone to Jeremy, the two sitting in the eerie silence of Nic the Nec's fuckery.

'Poor Sybil,' said Jeremy. 'Quite a character but a character who became too good for his own characterization.'

'Poor Sybil,' agreed Tone.

'It's very quiet in here,' said Jeremy mischievously.

'It is, isn't it? But that's to be expected with the old refrigerating cabinets being switched off.'

'Yes, very strange. They were off again for a happening that didn't quite happen, as you may recall! The person, hoping to take advantage of the slight thaw was somehow very pleasantly waylaid back in his flat.'

'But now they're off again?'

'Yes, this morning. I must admit I'm rather worried though about the contents getting well and truly beyond their *cell by* date!'

'Are the contents too far gone to be used then?'

'Nah! Only by a day or two. Want to give it a try?'

'Why not? Then, like all conscientious people we simply bin the rest.'

'Later, much later. A long, pleasant drive down to the coast perhaps, dropping off a few bin bags on the way?'

'Why not, it' a perfect night for a drive and we can have the top open.'

'Shall we?'

'After you!'

Pulling open the door to Cabinet 6 Jeremy slid out the tray containing Mark's naked corpse.

'Still nice and firm, not too iced up internally I shouldn't think.' murmured Jeremy showing off his expertise. He grinned up at a stony-faced Tone. 'The first time I tried this he was still a bit iced up inside. Could have resulted in a nasty touch of frost bite on my poor dick!'

'That would never igloo!'

'That, Tone!' said Jeremy with a grin, 'That was sad, very sad!' Jeremy gave Mark's pale chest a prod. 'Old Nic must have had an innate timing mechanism in his head. We'll get him turned over and do the finger test! Here. Help me lift him onto the table over there. I found it a bit high to start with but if you're careful and don't get too carried away, it's OK!'

'Why not the floor? If we're going to go wild we may as well be comfortable!'

'Why not? I'll get some bin bags. We'll be needing them later anyway.'

Having spread the bags on the tiled floor they reverently laid Mark face downwards on the plastic.

'Be my guest,' said Jeremy, eyeing the enormous bulge in Tone's jeans.

'I know,' laughed Tone. 'I was worried I wouldn't get a hard on but I tell you something jer, I can hardly wait to dip the prick!

'Pick, Tone, pick!'

'Why pick?

'As in ice pick, Tone! You may find it a chilling experience but I promise you, my friend, its cool!'

Three hours later the first bin bag containing Mark's left leg was deposited in a municipal rubbish dump near Slough. Half an hour later a second bag was clandestinely submerged in a bog on the estate belonging to the family of one of Jeremy's ex-school friend.

'I feel like fucking Santa Claus,' laughed Jeremy when, just before dawn and a long drive across county they had finally deposited Mark's head in a landfill near Brighton.

'And I'm so happy being Santa's little helper.'

'Not so little if I remember Santa's little helper's helping er… hand?'

'Sorry to disappoint you Santa, but I think it's true what they say, the cold *does* make you cock shrink and your balls shrivel!'

'Bullshit, my friend! By the time you'd finished fucking Marky, he was steaming!'

CHAPTER 17

An agitated Tiffany sat looking at a distraught Giles. 'I tell you Giles,' she said. 'Something's going on. And I have a very nasty gut feeling it's our Tone behind all this. I know you're upset about Sibyl and refuse to accept my theory that Sybil's death was *not* an accident. I believe it was deliberate! Cold, cruel and calculatingly deliberate!'

'Please, Tiffany!'

'No, Giles. *You have to listen to me*! It's that Spiers-Seaton syndrome all over again. Since our little upset at lunch I haven't heard a single murmur from Franchot "call me Tone"! Nor was I surprised when he did a no-show at David's funeral.'

'Well, it was pretty inconsiderate for Sibyl wishing to be buried up in that dreadful little Yorkshire town. At least Jeremy was there!'

'Well, he was Sybil's er... David's nephew.'

'And he did have the decency to invite us to lunch after the funeral. But remember, he also said he hadn't seen nor heard from Franchot.'

'It was pretty obvious he was lying!'

'Possibly, 'Giles gave a long, slow, sad sigh. 'So, Tiffany, dear, what now?'

'What now? Zilch, Giles, *nada,* nothing! I've had enough. It would have been an amazing ending leading to a brilliant new future but not all stories are allowed to have a happy ending. Life isn't Hollywood.'

'So what are your plans?'

'First, a long break away from it all and, if I were you Giles, I'd watch your back. You know too much.'

'I'm hardly going to spill the beans now, am I?'

'*I* know that Giles, but do our friends?' Tiffany stood up, giving the dapper, little man a genuine smile. She held out her elegant hand, 'I'm really sorry about Sybil, Giles. He was a fun guy and you two were good together.'

'Thank you Tiffany dear, and thank you for referring to Sybil as he. He would have appreciated that.'

'Goodbye Giles.'

'Goodbye, my dear.'

Walking up Cliveden Place towards Sloane Square Tiffany made a call. 'You ready for the grand finale? Good, because so am I!'

'Your bags packed?'

'Packed and ready to go! Christ Jer, talk about déjà vu! This is almost uncanny!'

'I *like* Malta,' laughed Jeremy, 'and I have fond memories of the pool at the Phonecia.

Like Tiffany, Jeremy and Tone had decided to leave well alone for a while. Francis, momentarily distraught on hearing about Sibyl's unexpected demise, was otherwise living happily in Paris. He had vowed never to replicate any other living artist's work 'ever again' and, supported by the devoted, doting Jean Claude, was determined to become the twenty first century Matisse.

'More Minnie fucking Mouse than Matisse!' had been Jeremy's only comment on hearing the news.

Giles they had decided to leave well alone and should it look as if could become a problem, as Tone said, 'Trevor's a real dab hand behind the wheel!'

The bond between Jeremy and Tone had gone from strength to strength, the initial experimentation with Mark leading to new horizons bonding them even more. The refrigerated cabinets went on to continue their strange habit of turning on and off intermittently while catering for a steady stream of visitors, some staying for only a few days with others a few weeks at a time.

A calculated cruising of bars and clubs made sure of a never ending supply of these unsuspecting occupants.

The unexpected discovery of Mark's head, a discovery which was still baffling the police, saw the two men making regular clandestine visits to a pig farm belonging to another of Tone's contacts from 'the old days.' The pigs had never been better fed.

MALTA:

'Whatever made us come up with such a bizarre idea in the first place,' murmured Jeremy to Tone as the pair lay side by side on their sunloungers facing the pool at the Phonecia, reminiscing over the past months.

'A momentary madness,' suggested Tone.

'But all's well that ends well,' laughed Jeremy.

'Christ!' said Tone, sitting bolt upright on his lounger,

'What?'

'That blonde over there!' He nodded discreetly in the direction with his chin. 'For a moment I could have sworn it was Tiffany!'

'Too much reminiscing, Tone,' laughed Jeremy. 'Besides, not only is Madam Tiffany a brunette, she would never allow herself to be seen dead in a place as mundane as Malta! And talking of reminisces,' here Jeremy couldn't resist another light laugh, 'I remember when our wine glasses were once full!'

'Touché!' said Tone beckoning the ever vigilant wine waiter.

'Fuckin' luvly!' said a harsh Australian voice, 'Fuckin' luvly! Great spot this place, fuckin' great! There's nuthin' to beat a bit of fuckin' culture! This Phonecia place, huh? Why, I feel I'm in almost fuckin' ancient Greece!'

'Jesus!' muttered Jeremy, 'just what we need, a bloody loud-mouthed Australian dick head. I thought we'd left that lot back in Sydney.'

'All he needs is a bush hat with a few corks hanging from the brim!' laughed Tone. 'Oh shit, he's coming over here!'

'G'day!' sang out the coarse Australian. 'Hope ya don' mind me coming over to say g'day to you two gents, d'ya?' He gave a now scowling Jeremy and stony-faced Tone a long piercing look. 'Handsome couple, hey? Coffee and cream!'

'Now look here…' said a red-faced Jeremy, ready to rise to his feet.

'Sorry, mate! No offense! Oops! My mistake! Better make my arse scare!' He waved in the direction of a blonde who in turn had been waving at him; the same blonde Tone had mistaken for Tiffany. 'The old groin's pointing! New bride, you see. Can't get enough of old Nev the Rev!' With that the foul mouthed man ambled off back to the blonde.

'Well, I can assure you we've had enough so no fucking groin-pointing again in our direction, if you don't mind, *Nev,* you spastic old cunt!' Jeremy gave a grimace. 'Coffee and cream! I'll fucking coffee and cream him if he ever gets near us and comes out with that gem again!'

'Forget it Jer. Finish that while I order us another bottle.'

Jeremy gave a yawn. 'Not for me, Tone.' He gave his companion a lewd wink. 'Fancy a siesta? Great! I was thinking of us driving up to Mdina this evening. It's that old medieval town up in the hills about ten kilometres from here. We can hire a car at the desk. I'm told there's a good little restaurant in the main square where can sit outside and have dinner under the old oleander trees.'

'Perfect!'

'Great, I'll go organise a car, a self-drive in case we get the urge *en route*, if you catch my drift!'

'I'll catch you back in our suite before then, equally *en route!*'

Having collected the car, a sedate Fiat, the two set off for the ancient hillside town. Tone, sitting behind the wheel, was humming cheerfully while Jeremy, with a mischievous grin, kept playing with the big man's rampant erection straining against the restraining linen stretching over his crotch.

'Christ Jer,' swallowed Tone, 'anymore of that and we'll have to stop.'

'Looks like we have to stop anyway,' Jeremy pointed through the windscreen to a car parked halfway across the narrow road ahead. 'Oh fuck, oh double fuck!' he muttered. 'It's that arsehole Aussie from the hotel! He was also hiring a car went I went along to the desk.'

'We'd better stop.'

'We've no alternative. His fucking car's completely blocking the road. Shit, so much for dinner beneath the oleanders.'

'Hold your horses, it's probably only something minor.'

Drawing up a few metres distance from the parked vehicle, the two young men slowly got out.

'Why, hello again!' called Nev, 'Our Knights of Malta in their fuckin' shining armour! Yer just in fuckin' time!'

As if seeing a tableau unfolding in front of them, Jeremy and Tone watched in growing consternation as a blonde, smiling Tiffany helped herself out from the back of the car while her companion, a veritable and extremely ugly giant, pulled himself out from the other side.

'Good evening, Franchot! Good evening, Jeremy! I believe you've already met my wannabe husband Nev – he should be so lucky! – but you haven't yet had the pleasure of meeting my *bona fide* husband, Howie. Howie Carpenter.' Signalling with a movement of her head for the large man to come and join her on her side of the car, Tiffany continued, 'Howie, come and say hello to Jeremy and Franchot – or Tone, both of whom you've heard so much about.' Taking the giant by his massive arm Tiffany spoke once more. 'Jeremy! Franchot! You two odious, vile excuses for human beings; say hello nicely to Howie before you say goodbye.'

ABOUT THE AUTHOR

Robin Anderson, an internationally known author and interior designer was born in Scotland and brought up in the former Southern Rhodesia (now Zimbabwe) and South Africa. Before attending Rhodes University (the Oxford of South Africa) he hosted his own radio programme in Rhodesia ('The Golden Voice of Teenage Half Hour!) and worked as a cub reporter on 'The Bulawayo Chronicle' during his gap year.

Leaving South Africa, he spent the early Sixties working with interior design companies in Paris, New York and London. He set up his own design company in London in 1970. Although interior design had been his first interest, the designer never stopped writing. Nowadays he makes numerous television appearances and is a regular guest on selected radio programmes, gives regular lectures on his writing.

His first novel, REGINA, A NOVEL OF SOME EXTREMES, was published in 1998. The novel gives a salacious look 'behind the scenes' of the glamorous but bitchy and competitive world of interior design, following the path of the unpleasant but talented Reginald Forbes as he cuts a swathe through the lives of his many unsuspecting victims.

Though London-based, the author travels extensively and the benefits of this are apparent in the various settings to his books. The Amazon, the Yucatan, Borneo, Myanmar, China, Russia, Japan, Sri Lanka, India, Egypt, Morocco, Kenya, Australia, The Maldives, Mauritius, Central Europe, Canada, North and South America plus the majority of the Caribbean Islands have also been visited. He has walked the Inca Trail in Peru; climbed Mount Kinabulu (Borneo) and Mount Kilimanjaro (Tanzania).

The author is a strong believer in the protection of endangered species. In 1959 he took part in 'Operation Noah' which involved the rescue of hundreds of animals from the rising waters of the new Kariba Dam being across the mighty Zambezi River in the north/western part of Zimbabwe.

He is also the proud 'foster parent' to four Orang-utans living at the famous Orang-utan Sanctuary in Sepilok, Borneo plus two elephants, Marlene and Marlon, who live happily on a ranch in Zimbabwe.

In a total contrast to the above, he also helped with the salvaging of precious works of art and manuscripts in Florence, Italy, during the Sixties when the Rover Arno burst its banks and flooded a major part of the ancient city.

In between his travels Anderson lives mainly in a spacious studio 'overlooking a glorious, leafy square' in London's exclusive Chelsea and a small hideaway in the Cinque Terre in his beloved Italy.

'Have laptop, will write and will travel!' is his mantra. **Bruised Fruit** is his eighth novel. In addition he has published a collection of short stories, **Thirteen Tales of Textual Arousal**.

ROBIN ANDERSON 2010
www.robin-anderson.com

A NOVEL BY
ROBIN ANDERSON

STILL
LIFE

ANDERSON

STILL LIFE

A BONER
BOOK

THIRTEEN TALES OF TEXTUAL AROUSAL

a selection of tales by

ROBIN ANDERSON

ANDERSON

THIRTEEN TALES OF TEXTUAL AROUSAL

www.ingramcontent.com/pod-product-compliance
Lightning Source LLC
Chambersburg PA
CBHW051127260626
47170CB00005B/1703

* 9 7 8 1 6 1 0 9 8 0 2 3 4 *